THE BLACKSMITH

James P. Barber

Also by James P. Barber

Hill of the Bear

Recollections of a Museum Collector

The Collector, the Guide and the Bone Digger

The Gifted Way to Manage Your Career

The Hilgendorf-Haag Connection

From New York to Indiana:
A History of the Ira Barber Family Beginning in 1786

The Blacksmith

James P. Barber

THE OTHER ROAD PUBLISHING

THE BLACKSMITH
The Other Road Publishing
630 Nancy Street, Warsaw, Indiana 46580
www.jamespbarber.com

Copyright © 2020 James P. Barber

Printed in the United States of America

First Edition, 2020

ISBN: 978-0-578-79451-8

Cover Design by James P. Barber

Other works by James P. Barber can be found at www.jamespbarber.com.

This book is dedicated to my maternal grandfather, Robert Charles Wendt, who was the inspiration for this story. Robert was the last working blacksmith at the Allis-Chalmers Company in La Porte, Indiana.

Like the main character of the book, Robert was an immigrant from Germany arriving as a child, although a little younger (age 3) than the main character of this story, Carl, and in an earlier year (1882). One of nine children, Robert was born near Berlin, Germany, in 1878. He became a naturalized citizen of the United States on March 1, 1922.

Also like the character of Carl, Robert was, unfortunately, an alcoholic. My grandfather passed in 1957 when I was heading toward nine years old, so I do not have many memories of him. I do recall, however, visiting his apartment, which was a tiny room above a bar in downtown La Porte.

My mother was raised by her father and an older sister after Robert and his wife were divorced in 1927 when my mother was three years old. I recall my mother relating to me that they were very poor during the Great Depression, and Robert only worked two or three days a week at the Rumely Company in La Porte.

The similarities to our main character end there. The rest of the story is fiction placed against the historical backgrounds of immigration, the Rumely and Allis-Chalmers companies of La Porte, and a German spy ring in America at the dawn of World War II.

Acknowledgments

I am grateful once again to the keen eye of my sister-in-law, Michele, who agreed to take on the challenge of editing my words. I am amazed at her ability to uncover and correct my misapplication of the English language. Thanks, Michele!

I also want to thank my wife, Marti, for her encouragement on this project. She appreciated this story more than my previous novel. I only hope that the first novel was not so bad in her eyes that anything would look better! I love you, dear.

Family means so much to both Marti and me, and I enjoy using family history as a foundation for my novels. We all have stories to tell, and maybe we tend to embellish them over time. With a novel, that embellishment can take one as far as desired to explore an exciting adventure. Thanks to family for providing inspiration in so many facets of my life.

Zillah also bore Tubal-cain; he was the forger of all instruments of bronze and iron.

Genesis 4:22, English Standard Version

Chapter 1

Somewhere in the North Atlantic Ocean,
April 1900.

The bow of the ship rose high in the cruel seas like a whale breaching out of the water, and then pounded back into the ocean as if hitting solid rock. The overburdened bulwark of the ship groaned in disapproval. With little delay, the process repeated itself again and again.

Low in steerage, the passengers were tossed about like a fallen crate of potatoes. The migrants cried and moaned as they scrambled to maintain their hold on the nearest post, bunk, bench, or body. The smell of vomit reeked as it mixed among other putrid liquids sloshing across the steerage deck in the cramped hold of the ship.

The family of the small, wiry German was separated in the melee. Ludwig Schmiedemeister held tightly onto his ten-year-old son Karl with one hand and tried to maintain his position with the other hand on a post that was clutched by numerous hands, arms, and bodies. Ludwig's wife had the two younger children, but Ludwig had lost sight of them.

Many who had been trying to speak only English were now crying out and praying in their native tongues. The mix of German, French, Russian, English, and many Scandinavian dialects created a cacophony to rival the confusion of languages surrounding the Tower of Babel.

Ludwig was able to maintain his position at the post as bodies collided and others went flying across the deck. While his grip on Karl grew slippery, his strength enabled him to keep Karl tightly clasped. He could only hope that his wife and the other children were safe from serious harm.

Karl tried his best to be brave, but tears flowed from his eyes. It was as much from being hit by people and objects as it was from his fear of the situation. He looked to his father for assurance that they would be safe. His father's eyes did not seem to display fear nor calm, but more a rage at being caught in this situation.

"Papa?!" the young boy screamed out, not for any particular need, but rather in question as to what was happening to them. But, the small voice could not be heard above the din in the overcrowded space.

While others around them spewed what little food they had left in their stomachs, Ludwig and Karl had not been affected by the motion of the steamer as it was tossed about in the violent seas. Still, they were covered with the stomach contents of others who were less fortunate when it came to the nausea caused by the agitated North Atlantic. Ludwig continued to scan the prison-like confines for the rest of his family.

Ludwig Schmiedemeister brought his family from their farm in Ganshendorf, Germany, several weeks earlier. He had been persuaded by an uncle and two cousins who had emigrated to America several years earlier. They told Ludwig of the available farmland and the opportunities that they experienced in the new land. They had settled in Wisconsin and encouraged Ludwig to do the same. However, they also told him of several German settlements along the way in Indiana and Illinois. They themselves had considered settling there, but they wanted to proceed farther west.

Ludwig saved for the next year to accrue the thirty American dollars for each family member for the ship passage. In addition, he was informed he must have at least twenty-five dollars for both himself and his wife upon arrival in America.

The small farm he worked did not belong to him, so he was not able to make any money from the sale of land. However, he was able to sell the farm tools he had collected over time. Those proceeds had provided him a little extra money over and above his minimum requirements to get into the United States.

After a week of travel from Ganshendorf and another week of waiting for the ship, the Schmiedemeister family boarded the passenger steamer *S. S. Gellert* at the port of Hamburg. It was smooth sailing from Hamburg to Le Havre, France, over the next three days. The easy progress of this early leg of their journey was the best thing that could be said about their travel.

The steerage passengers had been herded like cattle into the lower levels of the ship. They were pushed along with little regard for man, woman, or child. Any kindness and politeness of the crew was saved for the first- and second-class passengers. The passageways to the lower deck were narrow and crowded. Each person was carried along en masse blindly following those in front of them. Down steep stairs through low, darkened hallways into the lowest hold of the ship, they arrived in a crowded, sparse area. A narrow bench lined the side of the ship with small portholes. A few built-in tables were in front of the benches. Opposite the benches and tables were bunks in tiers lining the area from fore to aft.

Families scrambled to locate bunks enough for their entire group. There was chaos as pushing and shoving ensued. While they had been assured that there were more than enough bunks for everyone, the families clambered to ensure they would remain together in one area. Fortunately for the Schmiedemeisters, they were able to quickly move aft a bit and locate themselves together in a set of bunks across from a table.

Others continued to argue and shake their fists as they were shoved aside by the more aggressive travelers. Eventually, everyone found their space, and the arguing gave way to the sounds of babies crying, mothers disciplining, and children pleading. Coughing and moaning seemed to take on a language of their own with a constant din. There was little in the way of anyone attempting to greet their neighbor. Most sat quietly waiting for the ship to depart. There was an air of fear mixed with wonder at what was next for each of them.

Sailing was as smooth as could be expected for the first few days out of Le Havre. The weather turned quickly colder, however, as the ship steamed into the far north of the Atlantic Ocean. Huddled in steerage, the passengers were crowded in such a way that the wintry chill was not unpleasant.

Families began to speak to others as they fell into a routine. Most wanted to practice their English in preparation for entry into their newly adopted homeland. Sparse meals were even shared by some.

There were, however, groups of single travelers, mostly men, of course, who prowled about trying to display their virility. They began to taunt the weakest among the steerage passengers. They preyed on the most vulnerable demanding food or money as a bribe to provide protection.

When the storm developed, everyone was placed on an equal footing. All were tossed about without regard for age, gender, land of origin, strength of character, or health of body.

What had begun as some rough seas turned into a violent storm without warning to the huddled masses below decks. It was not unusual for the weather to act in this manner at this time of the year this far north in the Atlantic Ocean.

Queasiness quickly turned to fear and despair. The physically strong did have some advantage in maintaining a hold and keeping themselves with some semblance of stability. But physical strength was of little use to those with a weak stomach.

The storm lasted all afternoon and into the early evening before subsiding to mere rough seas. Those who were wrought with the worst seasickness were placed in their bunks. The others grouped together to begin clean-up, but the still rough seas did not allow even the simplest of tasks to be performed. At best, bunks were set up for sleeping. The moaning and heaving of the ill passengers made rest difficult for all, however.

Ludwig managed to locate the rest of his family. "Augusta!" Ludwig cried out at the first sign of his wife. She had suffered an injury to her leg and was sitting on the bench near a post with the children.

"Ludwig, mein leg!" Although holding the children tightly, she was in obvious pain.

Ludwig approached with Karl and reached out to help her stand. "Nein, Ludwig. I kahn nicht stand. Mein leg ist zu hurt. Take die kinder." Ludwig could see that she was exhausted from the ordeal and struggled to hold the two younger children.

"Karl, take dein bruder und sister to die betts," Ludwig ordered. He took the younger children by their hands and gave them to Karl, before turning back to Augusta.

Ludwig reached out to examine her. He began to lift her skirt, but she immediately stopped him. "Nein, Ludwig! Nicht here. Bring mich to die betts." She would not allow him to lift her skirt in the melee with so many others around.

Ludwig carefully lifted Augusta into his arms and staggered back to their berth. Once there, Ludwig covered Augusta with a blanket to examine her leg. It was not bleeding, but the knee was badly swollen and turning purple. Ludwig tore a strip from the thin blanket and tightly wrapped Augusta's knee. "Now, rast." His tone was more of an order than it was one of consolation.

Karl was with the younger children who could not stop their sobbing. Karl had wiped the tears from his own eyes and put on a strong face attempting to match his father's look of indignation.

Ludwig came over to the children, "Stop zu weinen!" The order to stop crying only changed the sobbing to whimpering.

Ludwig turned to Karl, "Care for dein bruder und sister." Ludwig returned to Augusta's side.

The weather broke before dawn, and some much needed sleep was obtained by many as children everywhere finally gave in to heavy eyes. The Schmiedemeister children had whimpered themselves to sleep with Karl in the berth next to them.

The next day was spent cleaning and gathering possessions. Most everyone was willing to assist others as needed. By the end of the day, order was maintained. The stench from the effects of mass seasickness remained strong in the hold, however, as the portholes could not be opened to let in any fresh air.

It was shortly after finishing the simple mid-day meal that Ludwig was approached by a young man. "Have you been able to gather all of your belongings?" he asked. While speaking with a slight German accent, he had, as most everyone, returned to the practice of speaking English.

Ever suspicious, Ludwig looked up at the young man quickly trying to assess him. He wondered why the tall fellow was not with his family. The youthful face of the young man was betrayed by deep, dark eyes that did not match the seemingly forced smile upon his face.

"We have everything, thank you." Ludwig, too, was again trying to practice his best English. His German accent, however, was much more pronounced than that of the young man. Ludwig returned to his activities reorganizing the family's belongings.

"I am just trying to offer some assistance to you. No need to be so disrespectful, Herr Schmiedemeister." He looked behind him at two other young men and smirked.

Ludwig looked up and noticed the other young men behind the first. "Again, thank you, but we are fine." He wondered how they knew his name.

"Oh, how many of you are there?" The young man attempted to sound interested in Ludwig's family situation.

Cautiously, Ludwig replied, "My wife und mein children." His nervousness caused his German to mingle with his English. He did not want to offer any details about his family. "You can move on." He looked down and away from the young man, avoiding eye contact.

The young man smiled, glanced at the other two, then returned his face to Ludwig. "Are you ordering me to move on?" He continued smiling, but his tone had changed to one of defiance.

Ludwig looked up. "Please, I am just trying to get our things organized."

The young man quickly interrupted, "And you want me to get out of your way? I offered to help you, your wife, and your three children, and you insulted me!" His voice was rising.

Karl approached his father from behind, curious as to what was going on. "Papa?"

"Karl, go back to deine mutter," Ludwig quickly ordered.

As Ludwig turned to Karl, the young man reached out and grabbed his shoulder. Turning, Ludwig was struck in the face by an unexpected fist.

"Papa, no!" screamed Karl.

Others in the area looked up to see the scuffle, but quickly averted their eyes not wishing to get involved.

The young man hit Ludwig in the face a second time as Karl looked on. Then one of the other two men grabbed Ludwig while the first man began rummaging through Ludwig's belongings.

"Halt!" Karl screamed as he lunged at the first young man. He was easily shoved to the deck by the bully who laughed at Karl.

"Stay put you little runt!" He lifted his hand as if to hit Karl, but he refrained.

"Now, you ungrateful little man, let's see what you have here." He rifled through the family's meager pile of belongings. "You call these old rags clothes?!" He continued throwing the belongings about the crowded space as Ludwig struggled and Karl looked on from his position on the deck. Augusta, with her injured leg, remained in her berth holding the two younger children.

Then the young man found a small, well-worn leather pouch tucked inside a tattered coat. "Well, now, what have we here?"

Ludwig struggled all the more, and the third man stepped in to help restrain him.

"No!" Karl leaped up from the deck and wrapped his small arms around the thief's legs.

This time the young brute did not hold back. With a look of contempt and annoyance on his face, he swatted Karl with the back of his hand sending him sliding across the deck.

His lip bleeding, Karl remained still on the floor, sobbing as he fought back tears.

Ludwig screamed and struggled to free himself. He had a look of complete terror on his face. "Ihr jungen bastarde!"

The thief ignored him as he opened the pouch and found a small brown package wrapped with string. Unwrapping the package, the thief saw a small stack of American currency. He laughed as he took the money in his fist and held it up in front of Ludwig's face. "Well, now you are showing your gratitude. Thank you for the money!"

Ludwig cried out, but he was struck several times about the head and slumped to the floor.

Karl wanted to do something, but he was frozen on the deck. His sobbing now turned to tears as he saw a movement from the corner of his eye.

Suddenly, the young man nearest Karl was tackled to the floor by someone flying across the room. This individual struggled briefly on the deck before one of the other men grabbed him from behind. The rescuer flipped the man over and pinned him to the ground next to the first man. He pummeled them both with several blows.

The robber reached out to the defender, turned him, and hit him squarely in the jaw. Unfazed, the new friend returned the blow. In the ensuing scuffle, the two other men scrambled away.

As the two continued to exchange blows, some of the money was dislodged from the man's fist. Not wanting to lose everything, he turned with the money he still had and quickly disappeared into the crowd, which frightfully moved aside to allow him to pass.

Karl ran to his father. "Papa, Papa!" He stood over his father who was moaning.

The hero knelt down to provide assistance to Ludwig. The young defender helped Ludwig out of his stupor and onto his feet. Karl hugged his father's leg.

"Danke . . . uh, thank you." Ludwig was both thankful and embarrassed. He had been unable to defend and protect his family. "Karl, bist du alright?" He showed genuine concern for his son. He wiped his son's face with his coat sleeve.

"Ja, papa, I am fine," replied Karl sobbing.

The young man stooped and gathered the money that had been spread across the deck. He held it out to Ludwig who took it gratefully.

Ludwig held out his hand. "Thank you for saving us. Was ist your name?"

"I am Robert Johannes. And you are apparently Herr Schmiedemeister?" Robert smiled at Ludwig who still had a look of fear, anger, and shame.

"Ludwig Schmiedemeister. This is my son Karl." He pointed toward the other side of the berth, "And that is Augusta and our two youngest children, Marta and Ernst." In his suspicious mind, Ludwig was even cautious of providing too much information to the man who called himself Robert Johannes. He also noticed that he spoke better English than most of the others.

"I am sorry to see what happened to you Herr Schmiedemeister. These ruffians and thieves have prowled about steerage looking to take advantage of others. They seem to have gotten bolder with each evil act. I am glad I came along when I did."

Ludwig felt his guard coming down a bit. "We have not much, so there is nothing I can provide you as a way to thank you. The little money we have left will barely provide for us when we port in America."

"Oh, no, you do not owe me anything. I was glad to help. Is this your first time going to America?"

"Yes, we left our home in Ganshendorf." Ludwig was becoming comfortable talking to the young man.

"Well, good luck to you. My parents came to America in 1890. I was about your son's age at the time. I am on a return trip after a visit to Berlin."

"Is America everything that I have heard? Is the opportunity as great as I have been told?" Ludwig was now anxious to hear what Robert had to say.

"Yes, you will be very pleasantly surprised, I am sure." He smiled and again held out his hand to Ludwig. They shook hands, and Karl actually saw a smile come over his father's face.

The man then reached out to Karl and shook his hand. "It is truly the land of opportunity, young man." He smiled and then turned and made his way through the throng of passengers toward the bow of the ship.

As Robert left, Karl realized that the hero had placed something in his hand. He opened his fist and saw a neat fold of American money.

Chapter 2

The Port of New York, Manhattan Island,
April 19, 1900.

An anxious fervor had overcome the steerage passengers as the ship arrived at the Port of New York. Everyone had gathered their families and their few personal belongings as they prepared to disembark. They were in America!

The throng of immigrants all looked forward to getting out of the stagnant lower holds of the ship and onto the main deck where there was fresh air. It was early morning, and they could hear the activity on the decks above them. Their spirits were lifted by the joyful sounds of those departing the vessel.

Over an hour later, one of the ship's stewards came down into the steerage compartment and informed the immigrants that it would be some time before they could depart. He also told them that doctors would be arriving soon to exam the passengers before they would be able to disembark from the vessel. He asked those foreigners who spoke English to ensure that the message was translated for others. He departed as suddenly as he had arrived.

There was a rise in the volume of the restless mass as the message was translated and discussed. Some were angry, some were disappointed, and some were just too tired to be either. Most returned to their bunks, while a small vocal group openly expressed their anger and shook their fists.

Ludwig and his family returned to their bunks where they set down their few small bags. Ludwig realized that in all the confusion, he had not been thankful for their safe arrival. He gathered his family around him and asked them to bow their heads.

He spoke in his best English, "We are blessed by God to begin our new lives in America. We are thankful for the protections He provided for us on this journey. We are safe and well and strong as a family. Thank you, God, for the rich blessings you have bestowed upon us. May we honor you in this new land in all our ways. Amen."

Karl was thankful, but he was puzzled by what his father had said. His father had been attacked and robbed, yet he thanked God for their safety. He wanted to ask his father about this, but he decided against it.

"Ludwig, how long must we wait to get off the ship?" Augusta asked the other question that was on Karl's mind. Of course, nearly everyone was wondering the same thing.

"We must be patient, meine frau. The man told us it would take more time." He also looked at Karl to be sure he understood. "We have been on this boat for two weeks; what difference does a few more hours make?" He smiled in an effort to make them see that he was not concerned.

By early afternoon when two doctors arrived in their area of steerage, the air was heavy from the lack of movement, and most were tired and discouraged. No one had provided any further updates on their status. The steward introduced the doctors and told everyone that they would be making preliminary health exams. Those who passed the exam would be able to get off the ship. Those who failed the exam would be taken to a holding area. He, again, asked for help in having his words translated. And, once again, the din of conversation and concern arose, but this time there was a higher agitation among the group.

Ludwig explained to his family what was going on, and assured them that since they were all of good health and had been properly vaccinated, there would be no problem. Karl clung closely to his mother as a sense of fear arose in him. Marta and Ernst were quietly sleeping.

They remained in their bunks as the two doctors made their way among the immigrants. About a half-hour later, a doctor approached the Schmiedemeister family. He asked to see their papers. He quickly looked them over and punched each paper. He did a quick examination of the children checking to be sure that they had been vaccinated. He felt their necks, looked in their mouths, and examined their eyes. He performed the same procedure on Augusta before proceeding to Ludwig.

His face frowned as he looked at Ludwig. "What happened to your face?" The tone the doctor used was somewhat accusatory. As he asked the question, he lifted Ludwig's eyelid with his fingers. Ludwig winced as the doctor's fingers caused pain to his swollen and bruised face.

Karl began to explain what had happened as the doctor looked at Ludwig's other eye. The doctor interrupted, "A fight you say? Is this something you are involved in often? Are you a trouble-maker?" His tone was biting.

Ludwig became defensive, "No, I am not a trouble-maker! I was attacked and robbed by a young man last week. Another man came to help me, or it could have been much worse."

Karl spoke loudly, "My papa is telling the truth. It was not his fault. He was hit by the man who robbed him!"

The doctor looked down at Karl then back up at Ludwig. "The bruises are consistent with what you say. I've examined your eyes for any sign of disease. You and your family appear healthy. You can also thank your son for his honesty in support of you."

There was a small hint of a smile on the doctor's face as his ticket punch performed its duty, and he told the Schmiedemeisters to proceed to the main deck with their papers. "Welcome to America," he said as he moved on to the next family.

From the ship, they were escorted by groups to the Barge Office. It was a short walk from the dock to the building. The Barge Office had been used as the immigration center after the entire Ellis Island facility had been lost in a fire in June of

1897. Construction was nearing completion on the rebuilding of the immigration center, but it was not yet ready to begin operations.

The family was guided from one line to another where they were questioned and evaluated more thoroughly than they had been by the doctor on the ship. Ludwig was questioned again about his injuries, but his entry into the country was ultimately approved.

The clerk who completed the final documents approving the family's entry into the United States had one final matter for the Schmiedemeisters that greatly disturbed Ludwig. The man said that Ludwig must change his family name for immigration as the Schmiedemeister name was too long and too foreign sounding. It would be best for the family, according to the clerk, to at least shorten the name. Ludwig did not know what to do. The man was insistent upon the name change. Ludwig did not want his family to be turned away after all they had gone through.

"Mr. Schmiedemeister, this is the best thing to do for yourself and your family. You are in America. It is best for you to do all you can to be a real American. Your name is a disadvantage to you and your family for your new future here."

The man looked up at Ludwig for an answer, but Ludwig was speechless. How could he deny his own family name? He looked over at Augusta. Her eyes were fearful and sad. "Ludwig, we must do this to be Americans."

The clerk had handled many similar situations. "Look, sir, why don't we shorten your name but maintain your German heritage at the same time? Say, something like . . . how about Schmidt? It is similar, but it is much easier to write and to pronounce . . . and it is more American sounding." He looked Ludwig straight in the eye waiting for his answer.

The moment seemed like a lifetime to Ludwig. Must he deny his own family just to be in America? He had heard of stories like this, but it had never entered his mind that this would happen to him as he could not believe such stories to be true.

Seeing the lack of decision, the clerk spoke, "Fine, then, Schmidt it is." Returning to his documents, he entered all their names using the last name of Schmidt. It was now official, they were no longer the Schmiedemeister family, but rather the Schmidt family.

Ludwig gathered his family and proceeded on dumbfounded. At the last station, they were directed to the railroad ticketing office as the next part of their journey was to be by rail to Indiana. Ludwig obtained the tickets for his family, but it would be the next day before they would be able to board the westbound train.

Leaving the Barge Office, the family was confronted with a need to find lodging for the night. On the street were numerous hawkers offering cab rides, money exchange, railroad tickets, boxed lunches, and room and board. Unfortunately, many of these were criminals or bribed immigration officers. There were even offers to purchase a certification for U.S. citizenship, albeit nothing more than a falsified and worthless document.

The Schmiedemeister family stood among so many fellow travelers, confused, uncomfortable, and even fearful in their circumstances.

"Ludwig, what are we to do until tomorrow?" Augusta expressed the concern. Her face showed the apprehension that was expressed in her voice.

"It will be fine, dear. We will ask one of the officials what we should do." He sounded positive but shared his wife's concern.

"Herr Schmiedemeister!" A voice called out from somewhere in the crowd.

Ludwig looked out as he heard the voice a second time. It was then that a young man approached the family waving his arms in the air.

"Herr Schmiedemeister, it's me, Robert Johannes, from the ship." He was aware that Ludwig had not immediately recognized him.

"Papa, it is the man from the ship, the one who fought off the bullies!" Karl was smiling from ear to ear as he was the first to recognize the young man.

Ludwig extended his hand as Robert met the family, "Herr Johannes. Ah, yes, I remember you; I could not forget!" They firmly shook hands.

"Where are you going for the evening?" Robert inquired.

"We will ask one of the immigration officials where we can stay for the night. Our train does not leave until morning." Ludwig's voice maintained an air of confidence, hiding his true feelings.

"Oh, Herr Schmiedemeister, you cannot trust any of the men out here who seem to want to help you. At best they will require more money from you than anything is worth, and at worst, they will rob you of all your possessions." He took a very serious tone with Ludwig as his eyes met with Augusta as well as with Ludwig.

"Look," Robert continued, "I am staying with a family friend only a few blocks from here. Come and stay with us for the night. He does not have a family, and he has plenty of room. I am sure he would be glad to welcome you into the country."

"We could not enter his home uninvited." Ludwig expressed his concern about proper manners. "It would not be right."

"Herr Schmiedemeister, I assure you it will be completely fine with my friend. Please, come along. It would be best and safest for your family." Robert was very reassuring. "In the morning you will be near the docks where you can take the ferry across the bay to the railroad station. Please, let us do this for you."

Ludwig looked at Augusta and knew that she approved of the young man's offer. Karl looked up to his father with eyes that longed for him to say yes.

"That will be fine, then. But, I insist we pay your friend a fair amount for lodging for the night." Ludwig was a proud man who would not accept charity.

"Then it is settled! We will share the evening together, and you can arrive fresh for your train in the morning."

Ludwig did not mention to the young man that his family had a new name. In fact, the thought had not even entered his mind.

It was as Robert reached down to pick up his own bag that Karl noticed he was missing a finger on his left hand. Karl wanted to ask him about the missing finger, but he thought he probably should not. Instead, he picked up his own small bag and joined the group as they headed up the street.

Chapter 3

La Porte, Indiana, 1906.

The Schmidt family had grown to nine with the birth of two daughters and two sons since the family came to America in 1900. They had settled on a farm just outside the city of La Porte, joining a considerable German immigrant population.

The county was mostly farmland, and the Schmidts had done well with their small homestead. It was hard work for all, but they had settled in with the community and appreciated all they had in their new home.

Being the oldest son, Karl, at age sixteen, took great responsibility with his father on the farm. He had taken a keen interest in tools and machinery, and he had developed into a very capable blacksmith in a very short time. In the past year, his skills were being sought by others in the area who needed repair work done.

For the Schmidt household, many Sunday afternoons were spent gathered with other German families at the beer gardens. With a sizable German population, La Porte saw a number of such settings. Families arrived following church services all dressed in their Sunday best.

The women gathered to share the latest gossip and current activity of their neighborhoods. They talked about their family circumstances, the work of their husbands, food preparation, child rearing, and the bounty of America. The wives made sure their husbands were getting plenty to eat while they let their children go off to play with their many friends.

Ludwig gathered with a close group of men who had decided their families needed to hold on to more of the ways of the old country. They felt like their way of life, their very traditions, were being swallowed up and lost in America. Surely, their very gathering at the beer gardens attested to the importance of preserving the German customs. They complained about the youth who were quickly falling into the laziness of the American culture.

Most of the men were farmers and factory workers who knew what it was to work hard. They recalled working on farms in their homeland when they were young. There were long, hard days, and never any complaining. Many of the men grumbled about their children spending too much time at school and not enough time working. Most felt that the children only needed the most basic education, and most of their time should be spent helping provide for the family.

Ludwig was not the only man with an older son who was trying to work his way off the family farm. He simply could not comprehend how a son could even think of abandoning his family. This would have been unheard of in the old country, but the culture of America was seducing them to abandon family and seek a way for themselves. The patriarchs of their respective families could only see the self-centered selfishness of such thinking.

Gathered with other young men about his age, Karl enjoyed the plentiful German food consisting of such main dishes as sauerbraten, schnitzel, hasenpfeffer, and bratwurst; along with side dishes of kartoffelpuffer, kartoffelkloesse, sauerkraut, and spatzle; and followed up with desserts like lebkuchen, apfelkuchen, and mohnstrudel. Of course, the German beer was not denied to the young men who did their best to display their bravado to each other and to the admiring girls.

It was in this arena that Karl learned to enjoy the heavy German beers. The beer was easily consumed with the well-prepared and heavily seasoned foods. Always with plenty to eat, Karl was never what one would call intoxicated. He enjoyed the food as much as the drink; the two just seemed to go hand-in-hand as part of his German heritage.

The one effect of the beer that Karl enjoyed was the way it seemed to open up his personality. He was a bit quiet and reserved by nature, but well into the afternoon at the beer garden, he was freer with his ability to carry on a conversation, especially with the young women.

Karl's handsomeness was not lost on most of the girls. They were often gathered in small groups on picnic blankets where they could be seen talking, giggling, and admiring the boys. Occasionally, a mother or two would approach and scold the girls for their silly behavior, but within minutes, the girls were again laughing, smiling, and pointing at the boys.

There was dancing at the beer gardens, and the women saw to it that their husbands danced at least a little. The men, however, would excuse themselves to relieve themselves or have a cigar, and rejoin their friends. The wives didn't really mind as long as they had at least one dance.

Far fewer of the younger people made their way to the dance floor. When Karl saw other boys ask one of the girls he admired to dance, he felt a tinge of jealousy. As relaxed as the beer made him feel, he just did not have the courage to ask any of the girls to dance.

Karl was standing with two other boys when a girl named Christiana approached him. Sure that she was heading for one of the other boys, Karl turned away.

"Karl?"

He turned around and saw her neatly bundled golden hair. "Uh, yeah. Me?"

"Yes, you," she said so sweetly that Karl felt he would melt.

"Oh, sorry, I just thought maybe you were looking for someone else." Karl felt embarrassed. He picked up his earthenware mug and took a long draft of beer.

"No. I see you here often, and I see you at school, but we've never spoken." She reached her hand out to Karl, "I'm sorry, I'm Christiana. My father is Friedrich Schirmeyer."

Karl looked at Christiana's outstretched hand, and hesitated before taking hold to shake hands. He was unsure how hard he should grasp her hand and felt that he had probably squeezed it too hard. "Oh, sorry. I work as a blacksmith, and I've got a strong grip." *That was stupid, Karl!*

"I know. You fixed a plow for my father earlier this spring."

Karl felt the confidence in her voice and demeanor. "Oh, yeah, I remember that. That was an easy fix. I hope your father hasn't had any trouble with the plow since." Karl found himself sincerely concerned about the work he had done. *Surely, Mr. Schirmeyer wouldn't send his daughter to deliver a complaint about my work.*

"Oh, no, everything is fine as far as I know; although, I don't see much of the plow myself." She smiled broadly at Karl.

Karl liked talking with her, but now he didn't know what else to say. Pausing, he took another draft from his beer stein. He wanted to say something, anything, but no words would form in his mouth.

Christiana kept the conversation going, "I understand your blacksmith work is quite good. My mother said that father thought you would have your own business one day." She paused for Karl to reply.

Alright, I can answer her question. "Well, I enjoy working as a blacksmith. But, my father's not pleased that I'm taking so much time away from the farm. He'd prefer that I stop trading my services to other farmers." Karl was suddenly feeling more comfortable in the conversation.

"But, Karl, what do you want?" Her head tilted slightly to the right as she asked the question.

Karl felt that she was really interested in his thoughts and feelings. He had never felt like this around a girl. He finished the rest of his beer.

Then three of his friends came up behind him and taunted, "Hey, Karl, are you gonna ask her to dance?!" They playfully shoved him, and then one of them handed him another mug of beer.

Karl was completely embarrassed and felt his face turning red. He looked up at Christiana just as one of the boys shoved him hard sending the full mug of beer into the air and onto Christiana's dress.

"Karl!" Her face showed disgust as Karl stood with his eyes and mouth wide open, unable to speak. After pausing briefly and waiting for Karl to say or do something, Christiana turned and ran off.

Behind him, Karl's friends were laughing uproariously.

"Hey, Karl, are you gonna run after your girlfriend?!"

"Way to go, Karl. You'll never see her again!"

"You better have another beer, Karl, if you want to face her mother!"

Karl's embarrassment turned to anger. He shoved his way past the boys looking for any way out of the area. He found himself at the beer tent where he grabbed a stein and quickly emptied it. He followed with another. He just wanted everything to go away.

Weeks went by, and Karl avoided the beer gardens telling his family he had picked up some extra work, which he actually did over time. His father admonished him not only for taking on the extra work but also for working on "Gottes tag," God's day.

The weeks turned into months, and Karl never did return to the beer gardens. Karl had been greatly affected by the incident with Christiana. His self-consciousness, especially around girls, was worsened by the event which he saw as caused by his so-called friends. He would never forgive them, and he would never talk to Christiana again . . . and he felt he'd probably never talk to another girl again.

Karl did find that the beer had provided him with a relief from the anguish he felt. More and more frequently, Karl found himself seeking comfort through the strong bockbier.

While most of Karl's days were filled with work, on those occasions when he was not as busy, he began to spend time in the local saloons. Guenther Brothers Brewery had a sample room on Main Street where he found some good German beer. There was a mix of old and young German men enjoying the drafts at Guenther's, and Karl felt he could easily fade into the background in this setting.

Karl was not like his father who became quarrelsome and combative when he drank to excess. At a certain point in his drinking, his father would find fault with everything. It was best for Karl not to try to defend himself, for that would mean a beating from his father. Karl had learned to avoid his father when he was in that way. If the barn was not far enough, then he would wander into the fields and woods to be alone.

Karl was nearly the opposite of his father. When drinking heavily, he became subdued and sullen. It was easier for him to talk to people in this mood, but his conversation was often quiet and sulky. It wasn't so much that Karl felt sorry for himself, it was more of feeling sorry for the state of the world around him.

However, Karl also became more generous when he was drinking. Perhaps it was his way of trying to make the world around him better. At Guenther's, Karl would buy drinks for his friends, and, often, as the evening wore on, he would buy drinks for complete strangers. Unfortunately for Karl, his list of supposed friends grew as his generous reputation grew. He was definitely being taken advantage of.

Chapter 4

La Porte, 1907 - 1909.

In recent months, Karl found himself spending more time performing blacksmith work for others than for his father on their own farm. Karl greatly enjoyed the work, much more so than the simple farm labor. He seemed to be finding his way as his own person as his skills improved and gained recognition.

His father was not pleased about Karl's circumstances, however. He appreciated the work Karl was able to do on the farm as the oldest son. He needed Karl, but he would not tell him so. Ludwig had grown even more proud, to his own detriment, and had become authoritarian in his demeanor, especially so with Karl.

Karl was just a few months from his seventeenth birthday and felt it was time for him to strike out on his own. He had recently approached the William Wegner Company concerning a position as a blacksmith. Located in the city of La Porte, the blacksmith company had been in business for nearly twenty years and was still operated by William C. Wegner.

Karl was confident that his abilities as a blacksmith would be able to meet the requirements of the Wegner Company. He explained about his experience beginning at a young age and the repair work he was doing for other farmers. He answered some questions, and at the end of his time with Mr. Wegner, he was offered a position as an apprentice blacksmith. Mr.

Wegner explained that if his skills proved out, he would be able to advance quickly.

The Wegner Company was one of only a few blacksmith firms left in La Porte. As production factories grew, there was less of a need for the blacksmith position. The few blacksmith companies remaining, however, were of high quality and in high demand.

Mr. Wegner had himself been an apprentice blacksmith for the William Pitner Company after arriving in La Porte in 1871. He learned the trade well, and formed his own firm in 1887 employing every scientific and up-to-date method in horse-shoeing, general blacksmithing, carriage repair, wagon making, and special order work. He and his company had a very good reputation in the community. He even had a company motto, "Not how cheap, but how good work can be done."

Perhaps it was pride, or perhaps it was shame, but Karl felt he should use the more common American spelling of his name. When it came time to complete the employment documents, he listed his name as Carl Schmidt. As he wrote this name, he recalled the time when his family entered America and had to change their name from Schmiedemeister to Schmidt.

The wage was more than Carl had expected, and he was excited to have the opportunity. But now, he would have to break the news to his father. He knew this would be difficult.

In their first year after arrival in America, Ludwig had been insistent in the family becoming what he called "good Americans." He expected them all to work hard, to learn and speak the English language, and become good American farmers.

And work hard they did. It took great effort to bring a new farm into production. It was a cycle of work, sleep, and work some more. As the eldest son, much more was expected of Karl. English was used at all times. This was not at all difficult for the growing boy as he quickly picked up the language.

But as the first year came to an end, Ludwig's demeanor changed dramatically. He had become engaged with a community of other German immigrants who were interested in maintaining their German heritage. When they gathered in one another's homes, they spoke only German. They read German newspapers and discussed news from Germany.

Eventually, Ludwig began to insist that the family speak German around the house and farm. Karl had no trouble going back and forth between the two languages, but his father became increasingly incensed if Karl let slip some English words.

His father had also become more of a hard taskmaster, expecting a greater amount of work from even the youngest of the children. Karl saw a fear being instilled in the smaller children as well as in his mother. He treated Karl differently, however. His father needed Karl on the farm, and he did not want his temperament to drive Karl away. But, his father had trouble dealing with Karl's time away from the farm performing blacksmith work for others. Karl had come to feel that his father likely knew that he would be leaving.

"Sie sind ein Idiot!" Ludwig lashed out at Karl in German. "Du bist ein egoistisches Arschloch! Sie würden Ihre Familie verlassen?!" Ludwig went on in German with numerous insults and ill wishes toward Karl. The more beer he had been drinking with his friends, the stronger were the German insults that Ludwig hurled at Karl.

Karl held his head high and tried to remind himself that his father did not mean all that he was saying. He let his father's rant go on until he seemed to run out of words. Then, all was quiet for a few moments.

"Geh raus. Get out," Ludwig said quietly. "You have your own life now." Ludwig turned and walked out of the room.

"Goodbye, Papa," Karl spoke in a quiet, now quivering voice.

Carl quickly proved his skills at the blacksmith shop. He worked hard and built a good reputation for himself. Mr. Wegner even mentioned to Carl that he reminded him of himself as a young apprentice. Carl quickly picked up on the inventiveness of Mr. Wegner and was envisioning his own ways of improving the work.

For the first year, Carl kept mostly to himself as he focused on improving his skills. He lived alone in a small room in town, and he was also saving his money.

Every two weeks, he would go to the farm and see his mother. His father was always busy elsewhere on the farm or with his German friends. Carl always left an envelope with some money in it for his mother.

After several months of impressing on Carl his need to join his co-workers and get to know them better, the small group of men convinced Carl to join them at a local saloon for a beer after work. Carl was somewhat apprehensive about meeting with the men. He knew them by name at work, but he had not really made any friends. He finally told himself it was time to change.

The men all told Carl how much they admired his skills. They even bought the first beers for Carl. The beer went down easily for Carl as it had been, as with most of the men at Wegner's, a part of their German life. Carl was able to relax and enjoy his time getting to know the men. Most of the men also came from German immigrant families. Carl felt a bond with them, and he thought maybe he could begin to understand his father's bond with the other German men.

But these men were different – they were not interested in their former country. They all felt that America was their home. This was a new place in which to have a new life with their own families. A couple of the men shared a story similar to Carl's relationship with his father. Their fathers had joined German-American societies that were focused on maintaining the old German ways and language.

Having had more than just a couple of beers, Carl felt his head spinning a bit as the men all said their good-nights upon leaving the saloon. Everyone was jovial, and Carl was feeling very good about his new friends. Carl walked a short distance from the saloon to the house where his small room was located. He was glad to be out in the fresh air.

The pattern became a regular one for Carl – work hard in the shop all day, then relax and enjoy the company of the others at the saloon before going home. One of the few single men, Carl found himself often buying drinks for his co-workers. He thought that since they had families to take care of, they would certainly appreciate the offer. His circle of friends seemed to be growing.

The nationwide temperance movement was gaining traction in La Porte as it had in so many communities across the country. Women played a strong role in the temperance movement, as alcohol was seen as a destructive force in families and marriages. A new wave of attacks began on the sale of liquor, led by the Anti-Saloon League. In addition, many factory owners supported prohibition in their desire to prevent accidents and increase the efficiency of their workers.

By 1908, "Blind Tiger" laws had been in effect in Indiana for a year. This law allowed for search and seizure of illegal saloons. A legal saloon had to have passed a two-year waiting period to obtain a liquor license. Many such "Blind Tiger" establishments were opening, especially in rural areas outside of the towns.

Fortunately for Carl and many others who still enjoyed their beer or hard liquor, Guenther's was still brewing beer and keeping a busy brewpub. There was occasionally a small group, mostly women, who would try to block the entrance, but, as at most drinking establishments, they were quickly ousted by the bartender who often chased them away with a broom.

With growing support, however, sixty-nine counties in Indiana became dry. But, the state was still unable to pass legislation for the statewide prohibition of alcohol.

Locally, support for prohibition gained traction, and some of the town's leaders were pressed into supporting the efforts of the Indiana Anti-Saloon League. Still, Carl and those who wanted to continue to drink managed to do so, albeit with a little more effort.

Carl's drinking pattern began to take its toll. Carl found himself not feeling well or being very tired on several mornings. He eventually showed up late for work. Because of the quality of his work, Carl was warned a number of times without any consequences. This only encouraged his behavior all the more. He was beginning to feel that his skills were such that Mr. Wegner would certainly overlook a few late mornings.

Over the next year, this habit continued. Carl was very focused on his work when he was there, but his attendance slipped even more. His absence at work was a common topic of talk among many of the workers. They were beginning to despise him because they felt he was getting special treatment.

More months went by, and the time came when Carl began missing work altogether. He was warned again, but he ignored the warnings as there had been no consequences for his previous behavior.

He arrived at work one Thursday afternoon after missing two days in a row. Mr. Wegner himself sought out Carl. With few words, Mr. Wegner let Carl know in no uncertain terms that his services were no longer required. He was fired.

It should not have surprised him, but Carl had become self-indulgent. He, of course, justified his actions as he needed to relax after working hard, and he was helping his friends.

He arrogantly felt that with his skills, he would not have a problem finding another job. But it seemed that the few local blacksmiths knew of Carl's drinking problem, and they did not want to take a chance on him in spite of his skills. This angered Carl, and he decided to remedy his feelings by drinking even more.

It was one such evening when Carl was at a local saloon that he stumbled and fell to the floor. A man who had been watching Carl helped him to his feet.

"Say, aren't you Carl Schmidt?" the man asked.

Carl swayed in the man's grip. His eyes searched for the man's eyes, attempting to focus on the man. "Yes, I am Carl Schmidt!" he loudly proclaimed. "Who is asking? Do you want me to buy you a drink?" Carl laughed.

"No, thank you, Carl," the man replied slowly. "My name is Fred, Fred Bluhm."

"Well, hello, Fred Bluhm!" Again Carl was very loud. "Say, why are you holding my arm?"

"You fell, my friend, and I am merely helping you to your feet."

"I did not fall, sir! Perhaps I was tripped!"

"Well, in any case, let me help you to a chair." The man eased Carl into a chair at a nearby table.

The man signaled with his arm and asked the bartender to bring two cups of coffee. "Carl, how about you have a cup of coffee with me?"

"Why, sure, Fred! Hey, how about a beer!" Carl laughed. "Sure, let's have a coffee." A waiter brought over the coffee and placed the two cups on the table.

"Carl, I'd like to talk to you about a job." The man spoke slowly and directly trying to look Carl in the eyes. "Would you be interested?"

"A job! Why, of course, I'd be interested in a job. You see, I am presently in the company of the unemployed man." Carl lifted his head and nodded at the man. "I am a very good blacksmith, by the way. You can ask anyone!"

"Carl, I know you're a good blacksmith. You're also a very intelligent young man based on what I've found out about you." The man paused. "Carl, you need a little direction in your life. I think a job at a very reputable company could help with that."

"Yes, a rep . . . repubab . . . a whatever you said, would be good!"

"Carl, let's get you home, and we can talk about this tomorrow. How would that be?" He smiled warmly at Carl, unsure that Carl would even remember this conversation in the morning.

"Yes, I think I am ready to go home." Carl swayed as he rose to his feet. The two walked out the door together.

Carl woke late in the morning and rose slowly from his bed. He sat up and let his head clear. He ran his fingers through his thick, dark hair and tried to recall the previous evening. Like so many recent days, he remembered looking for a job and then going to the saloon for a beer. He had met a few of his former friends from Wegner's and bought drinks for everyone. He recalled staying after they left, and that was about it.

He rubbed his face and noticed a piece of paper on the small table next to his bed. He picked it up and read a note, "Mr. Schmidt, in the event your recollection is a bit fuzzy, we met in the saloon last night. We spoke briefly, and I helped you to your room. As I said last night, I would like to talk to you about a job. Come to the Rumely Company at two o'clock this afternoon and ask for me. Sincerely, Fred Bluhm."

Through the cobwebs in his head, Carl recalled bits and pieces of the meeting with Fred Bluhm at the saloon. Yes, he had talked with him about a job, but he couldn't remember more than that.

He arrived at the Rumely Company shortly before two o'clock. He was led to Fred Bluhm's office. It seemed to be a busy office with people scurrying about carrying papers.

"Good morning, Carl," Fred Bluhm greeted Carl warmly. "Thank you, Emma," he said to the young lady who had shown Carl to Fred Bluhm's office. "Please, have a seat, Carl."

Carl sat in a comfortable chair in front of the austere wooden desk. There were few materials on the desk, and those that were there seemed to be neatly organized.

The previous evening now came flooding back to Carl. "Mr. Bluhm, please let me apologize for my, uh, condition last night. I'm afraid I had a little too much to drink." Carl looked sheepishly at Mr. Bluhm.

"Thank you for the apology, Carl, but let's not worry about that." He picked up a paper in front of him on the desk. "As I told you last night, we would like to offer you a job. I assume you are still interested?" He smiled at Carl.

"Yes, sir, I am very interested." Carl's enthusiasm showed.

"Carl, we've been looking at many blacksmith companies in La Porte and other communities as far away as South Bend." His tone was now serious and very businesslike. "We want to hire the best and brightest as we make plans for new machinery. We want men who not only have the talents of a good blacksmith, but who can also master new skills as our company progresses with modernization." He paused and noticed the interest in Carl's face. "I've spoken to your former employer as well as to many farmers in the area who called upon your keen abilities. You are very highly rated as a blacksmith, but even more, you show ingenuity and creativity in solving problems. You seem to have a good mind for conceptualizing solutions to problems. Do you feel this fairly describes your talents, Carl?"

Carl was stunned by Mr. Bluhm's assessment. He had never thought much about how he did things; he just solved a problem when he saw it. "Well, sir, I really never thought about it like that. I mean, I know I have very good skills as a blacksmith. I've often solved problems that others couldn't. I sometimes simply see the solution in my head and build it from there." Carl felt a little bit of pride, but he did not want to seem to be bragging.

"Carl, how are your mathematics skills?"

"I've never had any problems with mathematics. It seems to come easy to me."

"Carl, you're a young man, and the company feels you could make the most of your skills here. But, perhaps more importantly, we feel you could grow with some additional education in engineering. Do you think that is something that would interest you?" He set the papers on his desk and folded his hands waiting for Carl to answer.

"That sounds like a great opportunity. I never really thought about engineering, but I have thought about expanding my blacksmith skills into more refined areas. Yes, I am very interested." Carl found himself smiling broadly and eagerly wanting the job.

Mr. Bluhm smiled back. "Carl, you're one of the most talented young men we've looked at. I think we have a great opportunity for you." Now, there was a long pause. Mr. Bluhm spoke slowly, "There is one thing, however. Carl, you are a young man who has taken too much to alcohol. This is our biggest concern." Another pause. "Carl, I watched you all evening at the saloon. You spent your money too easily buying drinks for others. Unfortunately, you could not see how they were taking advantage of you. When they were all gone, you bought drinks for strangers. But mostly, you sat and drank alone. Carl, you are young enough to change this habit before it takes control of your life. If you can do that, then I think you would be an asset to the Rumely Company."

Carl's smile was gone, and he felt hopeless. He knew that everything that Mr. Bluhm said was true. He had known all along it was true, but he felt like a more important person when he was buying drinks for others, even if they were taking advantage of him. He could not even recall how he had gotten to this point. He was now nervous. Could he meet Mr. Bluhm's expectations of him? He suddenly had doubts about himself. *Who am I?*

"I'm sorry, I was just trying to relax with friends after work. I guess I get carried away a bit at times. Last night was not like most nights. I was feeling bad not having found a job and all." Carl realized he was making excuses. He knew Mr. Bluhm could see right through him.

"Carl, you know what you're doing, don't you?" He looked squarely into Carl's eyes. "I've seen you on other nights."

"Yes, sir. There are no excuses." He looked for courage to say more. "I'm not sure what to tell you. I see that I made some poor decisions. I would be a fool not to see that and not to change my ways with the offer you're making. Mr. Bluhm, I can be the employee – no, the man – you are looking for."

"I'm counting on that, Carl. Let's get some paperwork filled out for you so we can bring you into the Rumely Company."

Chapter 5

La Porte, 1910 - 1911.

By May 1910, Carl had been working at the Rumely Company for a full year. As he had done when he started his job at Wegner's, Carl put his mind to his work and was dedicated to improving his skills. Carl was determined to prove his worth and better his life.

There were a large number of workers of German immigrant families at the company. The Rumely family's business had been in La Porte since 1848 when Meinrad Rumely joined his brother John to operate a foundry. In 1859, they expanded the business into the production of corn shellers and threshing machines. Following the success with these new businesses, Meinrad bought out his brother's portion of the business and incorporated it as the M. Rumely Company by 1887. Starting in 1895, Meinrad expanded the product line to include steam-powered traction engines.

Meinrad died in 1904, but his sons continued to manage the business. Rumely's newest innovation, the kerosene-powered Rumely OilPull traction engine, was first developed in 1909 and began selling to the public by 1910.

When Carl started with the company, he was placed on a team of men that was developing the new OilPull engines. His skills as a blacksmith along with his ability to visualize and resolve problems had proven to be a great asset in the new design. At the same time, he was learning to read and understand the drawn plans that were used to develop the machines. He was happy with his work and devoted to improving himself.

When the OilPull traction engine was rolled out, Carl felt a pride along with the rest of the men on the team. Carl was called in over the next several months to make small changes to correct problems and enhance the machine.

Then, there seemed to be a lull in the work. The manufacturing facility was busy making the popular new traction engine, but Carl was no longer involved in the manufacturing line. His role was in the area of new development. As a result, there was no specific project to consume his focus.

As Mr. Bluhm had promised, however, Carl was able to attend some classes to develop his engineering skills. While new and fresh to him, the classes proved to be easy for Carl. Unfortunately, his ability to grasp new ideas and concepts quickly resulted in Carl having too much free time on his hands.

He decided to locate some of his old friends and see what was going on in their lives. One evening, he stopped by one of the local saloons that had been a frequent watering hole for many of the men, but he did not see any of his old friends. Carl drank a beer and left. He was proud that he was able to have just one beer and leave the saloon. He felt he was in control.

Several days later, he stopped at another saloon in search of his old friends. He met one former friend who was no longer working at Wegner's. They had a few beers while Carl inquired about some of the other men he had formerly worked with.

Carl left the saloon and stopped at another that the man had suggested as a place where some of his previous co-workers might be. Sure enough, Carl ran into three of his former co-workers. They were glad to see Carl, and they congratulated him on his employment with Rumely Company. His position at Rumely had been a topic for them when they heard he had taken the job.

Of course, they offered to buy him a beer. He felt he was still in control, and he would be rude to refuse the drink. They talked, and Carl sipped his beer slowly. Soon, however, there was another on the bar before him. That one went down a little quicker. Then there was another.

Carl got home under control, but he knew he had had too much to drink. He wound his alarm clock to ensure he would wake in the morning, then he laid his head on the pillow and went fast to sleep.

The next day, he told himself that what had happened the previous night could not happen again. Over the next few weeks, he avoided meeting the men. He tried to occupy some of his time reading the engineering books that were available at Rumely's.

Then, walking home one day after work, one of the men, Henry, hailed Carl on the street. He met up with Carl and asked him to go to the saloon with him.

"No, I've got to be to work early in the morning. You go ahead." Once the words came out, Carl felt in control.

"Come on, Carl, just one beer . . . for old time's sake." Henry prodded Carl in the side. "Hey, there's a new waitress there you should meet. She's quite a looker!" He now tugged at Carl.

Carl turned with Henry's tug. "Okay, but just one beer." *Yes, I am in control.*

"Great!" Henry kept hold of Carl's arm and led him away.

None of the other men were at the saloon, so Carl and Henry sat by themselves. Soon, the new waitress that Henry had mentioned came over to take their order.

"What can I get for you gentlemen?" She was polite, and smiled warmly at Carl.

Henry spoke up, "Just bring us a couple beers." He then continued, "Carl, this is the new waitress I was telling you about. Meet Anna." Carl looked up at the waitress. "Anna, this is Carl."

Henry smiled broadly at Carl as Anna leaned in closer to Carl. It was then that Carl noticed her blue eyes. They were stunningly bright, and Carl found himself staring. He could not look away.

"Hello, Carl." She spoke as though she were talking to a very close friend. "Anything else, or just the beers?" she asked with a bit of playfulness in her voice.

"Say, Anna, Carl's an old friend of mine. He doesn't get out much . . ."

Anna interrupted Henry in the middle of his sentence, "Well, I'm glad you boys are here tonight. I'll get your beers." Her eyes maintained contact with Carl's, and then she turned and left.

"What d'ya think, Carl, isn't she a beaut!" Henry wanted Carl's response.

"I must say, she sure has beautiful eyes. She seemed to warm up to me quickly. Not so much you, but, of course, you're married." Carl chuckled.

"You should ask her out, Carl!"

"Oh no, don't be setting me up." But Carl turned his eyes to watch Anna as she returned to the bar to get their beers.

Carl lost the little control that he had. When Anna returned with their beers, he knew he would drink his beer down so that he could order another. He wanted to see her and hear her voice. He was smitten by her.

Over the next few weeks, Anna was cheerful, almost affectionate, with Carl whenever he visited the saloon. She spoke more frequently to him and seemed to linger when taking his order.

Carl had grown into a handsome young man. He was thin and strong with a ruddy complexion. He had a full head of wavy dark hair that was always mussed just enough to provide an appearance of confident aloofness. He had blue eyes of his own, but they were darker than the bright blue eyes of Anna.

Carl was still the quiet individual he had once been, but really more so now. Since that time at the beer garden when he spilled his beer on Christiana – yes, he could still recall her name and see her face in his mind's eye – he had never felt any confidence around girls. But, when Carl was around Anna, she seemed to inspire him to be less reserved and more confident in himself. It was a new and pleasing feeling for Carl.

Carl, again, told himself that he was still in control. He understood exactly what he was doing, and he was getting to know a beautiful girl. He was buying beer from her, but he would have bought sawdust from her just to have her near him.

Weeks later at the saloon one evening, Carl asked her what time she got off work. He offered to buy her a drink afterwards. She consented, and they sat together at a small table shortly after ten o'clock.

She was easy to talk with and seemed to enjoy being with Carl. Over an hour had passed when she insisted she had to go home. Carl offered to walk her, but she said no. Carl wasn't sure what to make of that. He watched as she left the saloon.

Another week passed, and Carl had a day off and stopped at the saloon for a late lunch. Anna was not yet at work. He had really hoped she would be there. He finished his lunch alone and found a newspaper to read to pass some time.

About three o'clock, Carl noticed Anna walk into the saloon. He watched silently with a smile on his face as she crossed the room heading toward the bar. He wanted to say hello, but he admired her from afar for the moment.

She stopped at a table where three men were drinking. She said something to the men, then one of the men pulled her onto his lap. She giggled as the men laughed. The man on whose lap she sat pulled her in and gave her a kiss. She responded in turn, then said something to all of the men before heading to the back room behind the bar.

Carl was stunned by her actions, and he certainly felt jealous. He was unsure of what to do. He put the newspaper down, stood up, and looked toward the bar waiting for Anna to appear. But before she returned, Carl turned and walked out the front door.

That evening, he met several friends at another saloon. Henry happened to ask Carl if he had seen Anna lately. The other men perked up at the question, and began making comments about Anna's looks. It was all good playful fun until one of the men mentioned Anna's flirtatious nature.

Carl immediately went to her defense claiming that she was a warmhearted, caring person who did her best to serve her customers.

"Oh, she serves her customers alright!" One of the men jumped on Carl's comment. The other men laughed.

"What do you mean?" Carl pointedly challenged the man.

"Hey, you know what I mean! There isn't a man Anna doesn't flirt with . . . except maybe Henry here." They all laughed loudly. "Carl, everyone knows what a tease Anna is with the men."

"Ahhh, you just see what you wanna see. You mistake her friendly attitude for something more." Carl found himself struggling to defend Anna.

"Uh-oh, looks like Carl has his eye on Anna!" And again there was a round of laughter.

"Bartender, bring this man another beer!" shouted one of the men across the room.

"I'm just trying to defend the girl. She's just struggling to make a living like the rest of us." But, Carl felt his words lacking and their meaning lost on the men. He took the beer that was placed before him on the table and drained it.

Carl made it a point to see Anna the next evening. She was pleased to see Carl, and actually said so.

"Anna, I really enjoy being around you. I think you're so easy to talk to." He wanted to say something about how he had come to her defense with his friends, but those words would not come out.

"Carl, I find your quiet shyness attractive. I like being around you as well." She paused and looked deeply into Carl's eyes. "Why haven't you asked me out again?"

"Anna, I see you in here being so playful with the other men. I'm not sure how you feel about me, and I'm not sure how you feel about the other men." Carl felt himself turning warm as his face reddened.

"Oh, Carl, that's just my personality. You know that. And, anyway, it's good for business to have the men buy me drinks." She smiled broadly at Carl, then leaned over and gave him a kiss on his cheek. "I'll be back, I have to turn in these orders." And she quickly disappeared into the kitchen.

While Carl spent more evenings at the saloon in order to see Anna, he did not let his drinking affect his work. He made sure to be at work on time every day, and he put in a full day's work, often working more hours than most of the other men.

One evening when he was out with Henry and his other old friends, they began to tease him about his relationship with Anna. The beers flowed freely as the men made sure to get Carl drunk. They knew they could get his goat once he had a few too many beers.

As Carl lost his inhibitions, he became bolder and louder, eventually challenging the men. Soon, things were said between Carl and the others that developed into something far beyond any good-natured poking at Carl.

Carl had had enough of it, and he flipped over the table, grabbed one of the men by the shirt, and punched him squarely in the face knocking him to the ground. Another man tried to pull Carl back, but Carl turned and threw a fist at him as well. The man was ready, however, and Carl's punch swung high into the air.

Unfazed, Carl turned back and hit the man in the head from behind. He did not go down but turned and faced Carl. His response was quicker than Carl's, and this time Carl went to the ground.

"Carl, stay down!" the man shouted.

Carl, bleeding from his nose, struggled to his feet. By that time, the first man Carl had punched dove into Carl, and the two flew back into the bar. Now, both men punched Carl. Carl was unable to fight back. The two men beat Carl until he dropped to the floor in a lifeless slump. He was out cold and bleeding from his nose and mouth.

"Dammit, Carl!" the first man shouted, "what the hell is wrong with you?!" He rubbed his knuckles as he turned away. The other men laughed at Carl and shook their heads as they left the saloon.

Henry remained behind to assist Carl. He poured a pitcher of water over Carl's head. This revived Carl, who shook his head back and forth.

"Take your friend and get out of here! You're lucky I don't call the cops!" the bartender shouted orders at Henry.

Anna had been in the kitchen but entered the bar area when she heard the shouting. She looked shocked when she saw Carl's face. She didn't know whether to be angry with Carl or to feel sorry for him. She noticed a number of people laughing at Carl's antics.

"Jack," she said to the bartender, "my shift is nearly over. Let me get him home." The bartender threw up his hands and then nodded to her in approval.

Anna and Henry helped get Carl to his feet. "Henry, help me get him to my place. I'll take care of him." The trio exited into the cool night air.

Chapter 6

La Porte, 1914.

Carl and Anna had been married just over two years, and they had two daughters, Marie and Rose. They were living in a small house in a mostly German neighborhood on the south side of La Porte. The two girls shared the second bedroom in the two-bedroom house. It was a simple home in need of a few repairs that Carl had been diligent about in the first year of their settling into the house.

They had little contact with any of their neighbors as they both worked long hours. Anna's mother lived nearby and watched the children when the couple's work shifts overlapped. Anna had insisted that they find a home near her mother. Carl was discovering that her reason was not so much because of a closeness to her mother, but rather so her mother could easily help care for the children.

Carl went to work early in the morning, and he usually got home about seven o'clock in the evening. Anna worked four nights a week at a downtown restaurant and beer hall. Depending on her shift, she may or may not be home when Carl got home from work. The times when they were home together seemed to be taken over by the attention needed by the two young girls.

So, most nights, Carl took care of the children. Most days, Anna's mother took the children so Anna could sleep. Anna was more frequently taking the late shift that closed the business and resulted in Anna getting home after midnight.

Anna had briefly become more settled after their marriage. She spent more time at home taking on the role as Carl's wife. She prepared meals and listened to Carl talk about the events at work. At times, they discussed what was going on in the world as reported in the newspapers. She even professed an interest in the repairs Carl was making to the house. Her real interest, however, was in having the home more presentable to any of her friends who might see it.

Anna had gotten pregnant before they married. Not long after their first daughter was born, Anna was again pregnant. Carl loved his family, and he felt hard work was the means to provide for them. At the same time, he looked forward to spending his evenings caring for the girls.

Anna missed going out to the saloons with Carl. When they were first married, they went out often. Carl did everything he could to ensure Anna's happiness. She would sometimes flirt with other men, but Carl felt it was simply her personality, and nothing more than innocent behavior.

With the arrival of the second baby, there was more time spent at home and less time going out. They both found themselves drinking at home more frequently. Carl had taken to drinking hard liquor more often than beer. The two of them often drank late into the night when they had days off together. Occasionally, Anna's mother took the girls so they could have a night to themselves. But, Carl wanted to stay home, and Anna wanted to go out.

Eventually, Anna told Carl she was working five days a week. It was partially true, as the restaurant manager allowed her to work two hours around suppertime in the beer hall. After that, Anna remained at the hall and drank with her friends, while enjoying the company of other men.

Carl felt energized by his work at the Rumely Company. He loved developing his thoughts into plans, and plans into actual devices and products with the skill of his hands. It was fulfilling in a way that not much else in his life was at the present time. He felt that he and Anna were becoming distant, so the opportunity to get lost in his work was very appealing to him and provided a sense of accomplishment and pride.

From his beginning at Rumely, Carl had been teamed with a small group of workers developing new products. While simply a blacksmith, his role on the team went far beyond that. His input was valued and appreciated. Once again, he simply felt he was doing his job.

He completed additional mechanical engineering training which he put to good use. His skills as a blacksmith were remarkable, but he was now beginning to work on more detailed mechanically engineered and machined parts. He saw machining as a mere refinement of the blacksmith trade. It all seamlessly made sense to him, and he easily adapted his skills.

His supervisors certainly recognized Carl's abilities. If there was a problem with an existing part or product, they would take it to "The Blacksmith" for an opinion, and often a final solution. If a prototype for a new part or product needed to be developed, again, they could count on Carl, The Blacksmith.

He had become fondly known as The Blacksmith by nearly everyone in the company. He was not the only blacksmith, but he was the problem solver with a gift to see in three dimensions in his mind. It seemed he could take any idea and develop it to fruition, often with improvements to the original design. When someone had a manufacturing or product problem they could not resolve, they called upon The Blacksmith.

Regardless of the actual requirements of his occupation, something he easily adapted to, he was still known as The Blacksmith. While his blacksmith activities were shrinking and his machine skills were advancing, he did not mind at all being referred to as The Blacksmith. It was a term of endearment which he found left him with a feeling of achievement.

While the recognition was not lost on Carl, he did not work for that recognition. He worked because he enjoyed it, and he enjoyed being of service to others. He just felt he was doing the right thing helping others solve their problems. Unfortunately, he was blind to the complications developing at home.

On the now rare occasions when he was working at his anvil, he would often recall working on the farm with his father. Unfortunately, his father had never forgiven him for leaving the farm. While Carl had at one time visited the farm on a regular basis to see his mother, he had not been there in years. His mother had died just after Carl's first daughter was born. His brother Ernst was still helping his father run the farm with his two younger brothers.

The only contact with his family that Carl now had was an occasional visit with Ernst. Ernst was busy with his own family, and Carl and Anna seemed to have no time to do anything outside of their new family. The cultural closeness of the German family had been lost in building their individual lives in America.

There were nights when Carl went home feeling a longing for his family, for a look of approval from his father. On those nights, Carl found himself pouring glass after glass of whiskey to push those thoughts and feelings away.

When Carl was not drinking to suppress those thoughts, he drank to forget the thoughts he had of what Anna might be doing at the restaurant. He knew she was a flirt when he married her, but he thought she would change after their marriage. He felt she had adapted to life as a married woman and a mother, but then she began to spend more time at the beer hall. She said they needed the extra income, but they didn't really.

Carl could not bear the thought of her flirting with another man, maybe even kissing another man, so he tried to drown out those thoughts with drink. Carl was coming to rely heavily on the bottle to get through most nights.

As much as Carl was drinking, he always managed to be up in the morning to be on time for work. His production efforts did not seem to suffer as far as he could tell. He was still doing what was expected of him, and more. At some point, he began to feel that his drinking was even helpful in his job as it allowed him to put out of mind those other thoughts that might distract him. He convinced himself that he was more in control than ever.

Chapter 7

La Porte, 1917-1920.

The new year brought about many changes in Carl's life. Just two years prior, the Rumely Company had been reorganized and was now the Advance-Rumely Company, so named after the acquisition of several other businesses, including Advance Thresher of Battle Creek, Michigan. The final reorganization under the new name was completed in 1915.

During this process, many, including Carl, worried about the status of their jobs, never really knowing from one week to another if they would be "reorganized" out of work. The Advance Thresher Company produced similar types of threshing machines and traction steam engines. One of the goals of the merger with Advance Thresher, as well as the acquisition of a number of other smaller companies, was to streamline the business while at the same time increasing production.

Despite all of the history and diversity in farm implement manufacturing acquired along with all of their corporate assets over the last five years, most of this was left by the wayside as Advance-Rumely Company sought to fold everything under its new brand name.

Progress in the manufacturing process brought about by such notables as Henry Ford and Harvey Firestone had been integrated into most factories, including Advance-Rumely. As automation continued at an increasingly rapid rate, Carl became concerned about his role as a blacksmith, even though his work involved much more than simple blacksmithing. He saw many other men, including other smithies, lose their jobs with the process innovations, as well as the acquisitions and reorganizations, in the affected companies. Fortunately for Carl, his position as a recognized innovator within a forward looking engineering and development group, kept him employed. But, still, like so many others, he was unsure of his future employment with the newly organized business.

Meanwhile, there were other pressing challenges for Carl and for many of the workers at the Advance-Rumely Company. These encounters took a more ominous tone as threats, threats to German immigrants all over the country, and threats to the German population at home in the town of La Porte.

Prior to the outbreak of the Great War in Europe, an anti-German sentiment was forming in America. When America entered the war in 1917, it became the World War, and anti-German sentiment became much worse. Every man with a German surname was under suspicion by his neighbors. In some of the larger cities, there were near riots against German immigrants.

Those immigrants with ties to family members remaining in Germany were especially vulnerable. They were seen as sympathetic to the German aggressors, when in reality, most of them were simply watching out for the well-being of their far-distant relatives.

The Advance-Rumely Company was founded by Germans, and it was a large employer of German immigrants in LaPorte County. Fortunately, the company did not support any of the anti-German propaganda, and, in fact, it worked hard to support the German population in LaPorte County.

Outside of work, however, things were a little different. In many everyday activities, the local Germans were often referred to as "Huns," a derogatory term from the Middle Ages for barbaric raiders who spoke a foreign language. Most of Carl's friends were of German origin, typically second generation in America, and few spoke German in any public setting. Even so, they found themselves cautious when out in the community.

Some Germans were fearful to the extent that they were changing their surnames. This made Carl recall the time of his own family having their name changed upon entry into the country. But, under the current circumstances, even Schmidt was considered a pure German name. Very few men in Carl's circle were even considering changing their names, but one suggested Carl ought to change his name to Smith as it would fit with his occupation. At least outwardly, it was all taken as a joke by the men.

Still, the men felt the stares and isolation in the saloons they had been frequenting for many years. They could by no means discuss the war in Europe. The worst thing they could do was oppose the war. That would certainly make them appear to be sympathizers with Germany. Saying nothing about the war placed them under suspicion of secretly supporting Germany. And, even those who outwardly supported the war against Germany were suspected of really supporting Germany under the ruse of supporting the war. It was certainly a situation that left the German immigrants in a bad position.

On one night, a group of men worked its way through Carl's neighborhood shouting threats and insults, and painting degrading words and symbols on the houses. No one dared approach the group, and most, including Carl, turned out their lights and cautiously watched from a secluded window. It seemed that once the group had puffed its chest and made its feelings known, there were no further incidents.

There were a few other obvious signs of the anti-German feelings. Gone were the German language newspapers. Carl had not read one since he had left home, but there were still some older men who read the newspapers. No longer. And, in the local schools, German language classes were eliminated.

Carl mostly ignored the talk and the stares, and he continued working hard at Advance-Rumely. Anna, meanwhile, continued working nights. She had begun using her maiden name of Gray a few years ago so she would be seen as a true American. What most people did not know about Anna was that her real name was Anna Grauberger. Yes, she was German herself, but no one knew it.

Anna's parents had come to America in 1886. The family settled on a farm in the northwest part of LaPorte County where Anna was born in 1893.

Anna never liked life on the farm, and after running away several times, she left for good when she was sixteen years old. She left the past behind her and never looked back. She did not talk to her family until her father died. Her mother was then able to slowly work her way back into Anna's life.

Anna's first job was waiting tables in a small restaurant in La Porte. The work was not hard, and she enjoyed talking with the patrons. She easily warmed up to people, and effortlessly made friends. Her "friends" eventually realized that she was only using them. It never bothered her when they left; she just looked for someone else to take advantage of.

It started small. She occasionally took some of the customers' change. Later, her impropriety became larger when she began to boldly steal directly from the cash register. She was caught and fired.

Her next job was at a small saloon often frequented by workers from the Rumely Company, as well as from other local businesses. As at the restaurant, she was friendly to the customers. At the saloon, however, her friendliness went further as she openly flirted with the men. Even the married men appreciated the attention she gave them. She often convinced the men to buy her drinks and meals. The owner, of course, appreciated this extra business, and Anna benefited from the tips.

With the extra gratuities and the attention of the men, Anna had stopped her stealing. It was much easier, she felt, to play on the kindness and attraction of the men, to seduce them. Some kind words, a touch, a look, or a dance, and she would be able to get what she wanted.

It was under these circumstances that she met Carl. Carl was different, however, and she saw him as a challenge. He was much quieter than the other men. He seemed more interested in his drink than in her. She wanted to win him over. It eventually led to a mutual attraction between the two. She had more than won Carl over and was satisfied with her victory.

The marriage seemed like the ultimate win for her. But, the marriage was just part of winning the game to Anna. She felt like she could, and should, marry Carl. It seemed to be the right thing to do. And, the first year was fun with Carl.

After the initial joy of being a mother, Anna saw before her a life that she was not sure she was ready to accept. Following the birth of her second child in 1913, she was more sure than ever that she needed the fun-loving freedom of her old ways. She needed to be around the men at the bar. She needed to be seen as a challenge to the men. She needed to be the tease that she had once been. She needed to be the center of attention. These were the things that made her feel alive. Life with Carl was the right thing, but her former life was the exciting thing that she desired.

She was sure she could manage both. She could flirt and dance with the men and let them buy her drinks. It did not have to be more than that. Then she could go home and be the wife and mother. She really thought she was balancing the two lives, but she was not. Her mother was taking the children more frequently. Anna was spending more time working, and she was seeing less of Carl.

Although their marriage became less stable through the next few years, they did have a third daughter, Leona, in late 1917. Anna pretended to be happy about the new baby, but inside she saw the child as a new obstacle to her ability to have her own self-indulged, intemperate life. She lacked any instincts for motherhood, and happily turned the mothering aspects over to her own mother. This was not lost on Carl, and he did all he could to more dearly love his daughters.

Things once again changed for everyone on April 6, 1917, when the United States government declared war on Germany. Anti-German sentiment reached a new high across the country. President Wilson, who, during his 1916 presidential campaign, declared that hyphenated Americans were potentially disloyal, proclaimed that all German citizens were "alien enemies."

This had the greatest effect on Germans in larger cities. The alien enemies were banned from living near military bases, near airports, or in the nation's capital. By 1918, these designated alien enemies had to register with the government and be fingerprinted. Those who failed to comply could be subject to confinement in an internment camp for the duration of the war. Carl, along with the other German men at work, dutifully complied wanting to ensure everyone that they were loyal to America.

Carl had to carry with him at all times the small four-page booklet that identified him as an alien enemy. If he were asked to present his registration and he did not have it, he was subject to arrest and detention for the period of the war. The booklet contained his name and address along with a photograph, his signature, and his fingerprint. Travel outside of La-Porte County would require a specific request and approval by the local law enforcement. Carl detested the reference as an alien enemy.

All of this stirred up the past feelings of Carl's arrival in America and his father's growing dissatisfaction at the loss of some of their German heritage. His father had grown bitter over the years, and he spent more time with other German men who felt the same. Carl could not recall his father speaking in anything but German up until his death in late 1916.

Only now did Carl feel that he understood some of what his father had experienced. Carl felt every bit loyal to America, but he also felt a growing resentment at being singled out as a

German. So-called patriotic organizations across the country were producing hateful anti-German propaganda under the guise of supporting the "true American." These organizations claimed that true Americans did not use any language other than English, did not read foreign-language newspapers, did not attend foreign-language church services, did not belong to clubs encouraging German customs, and did not criticize the government.

As the war effort developed, these organizations seemed to thrive on spreading fear of the Germans in America. Their propaganda warned neighbors to be watchful of German spies in their very own neighborhoods.

Carl's attitude grew worse as the war continued and he felt as though he had to hide his true identity. His own thoughts were mixed with thoughts that had been instilled in him by his father. He made it much worse in his mind than it was. In the small town of La Porte, the worst of the anti-German senti-ment did not manifest itself. There were a few loud-mouthed "true Americans," but it was relatively calm in La Porte com-pared to the larger cities.

In addition, Advance-Rumely Company was a respected business, not only in the community, but across the country. With the war effort, their production of machinery was in-creased, and many saw the men, even the German men, work-ing at the company as providing loyal support to the country's war effort.

Carl's confused feelings drove him to spend more time at the saloons, and when not there, drinking heavily at home. Many mornings he awoke in his chair where he had passed out, usually an empty bottle nearby.

Through all of this, Anna and Carl grew farther apart. She did not want to be dragged down by Carl's mutterings about his German-American heritage and his loyalty. So, she spent more time at the restaurant and beer hall where she could laugh and dance through the night.

In April of 1918, Indiana passed a statewide law prohibiting the production of alcohol while waiting for the states to ratify the Eighteenth Amendment to the Constitution prohibiting alcohol nationwide. The temperance movement had been effective in the state as Indiana became the twenty-fifth state to go dry. The approach by those wanting to ban alcohol had been effective this time around. Grain, they argued, needed to be preserved for the war effort. It was the state's patriotic duty to support this effort.

Many local saloons continued to sell alcoholic beverages in defiance of the law, including Guenther's owner, Fritz, who had been arrested several times for selling liquor. The Guenther Brothers Brewery was one of three breweries in town, and they seemed to find a way to keep business going through the support of their patrons.

In January of 1919, the Eighteenth Amendment to the Constitution of the United States was passed by the thirty-sixth state making prohibition of alcohol the law of the land. In October of 1919, the Volstead Act was passed which allowed enforcement of the Eighteenth Amendment, and on January 16, 1920, Prohibition officially began in the United States.

Many of the larger beer producers opted to produce non-alcoholic beverages or turned to other products. Many smaller brewers, however, continued to produce their goods secretly. And, for those who so chose, individuals began making their own liquor in the form of "bathtub gin" in their bathtubs at home.

Carl and other regulars at Guenther's brewpub were able to continue to drink at the private saloons, now known as "speakeasies," so named for the practice of speaking quietly about such a place in public, or when inside it, so as not to alert the police and neighbors. There were occasional raids by the police, but the speakeasy would quickly open again in another location. Carl had no inclination to make liquor in his own bathtub, although he knew some men who did. More often now, he was purchasing illegal whiskey and taking it home.

To satisfy the town's leaders, the local police chief led a posse and raided Guenther's brewery and smashed the kegs of beer with axes. It made great front-page news, but they were open for business a week later.

With ever-increasing raids on, and shut-downs of, speakeasies around the county, patrons moved their drinking into more discreet speakeasies, private halls, and clubs. These drinking locations became more expensive with the greater enforcement of the prohibition laws. As a result, many working class men turned to alternative forms of alcohol, not all of which were safe.

Alcohol was an important industrial chemical produced for paint solvents, antifreeze, embalming fluid, and other poisonous substances. Known as denatured ethyl alcohol, along with deadly methyl alcohol, these substances found their way into beverages. Many people got sick, and some died from tainted alcohols.

Finally, there was a loophole in the Volstead Act that allowed for the sale of medicinal whiskey. Sold through pharmacies, sales of medicinal whiskey sky-rocketed during Prohibition. Fortunately for Carl, he was still able to purchase bootleg whiskey.

Chapter 8

Milwaukee, Wisconsin, 1920.

He was older than most of the new prospective agents in the class at the Milwaukee office of the Federal Bureau of Investigation. He had grown up on a farm in Janesville, Wisconsin, the son of German immigrants. The first wave of German immigrant families had been welcomed there by the local English Puritan population. Many families wrote back to relatives in Germany with enthusiasm about the welcoming friendliness of the small town. As a result, even more German homesteaders settled in Janesville and the surrounding farmland with later waves of chain migration.

The forthcoming agent had wanted to be in law enforcement as far back as he could remember. He had an uncle who was a local sheriff in Janesville. He was a strong-willed man who Robert had always looked up to. He was rough around the edges and a little gruff, but Robert admired his strength and fairness.

His uncle was able to get him a job as a deputy in Janesville after Robert's graduation from high school. Robert had a strong sense of service, and he became respected by nearly everyone in town. He was known to be strict, but always fair. Many of the men in town thought of him as a refined version of his uncle.

There was not much crime for Robert to solve in the small rural farming community. He mostly dealt with minor issues, often involving an escaped farm animal or truant student. The occasional drunk was brought to the jail to sleep it off overnight. But, Robert felt he was performing a service for his community, and he was often the town's most outspoken advocate.

Robert spoke with his uncle about pursuing a long-term career in law enforcement and desiring to be part of a larger department. He told his uncle that he would consider working in Madison or Milwaukee to move up and gain more experience in "real" law enforcement.

His uncle made some inquiries on Robert's behalf. The news for Robert was a little disappointing. The department in Milwaukee was taking new recruits, but the new recruits were expected to have a college degree if they anticipated any opportunities for advancement. Sure, they would take a non-college recruit, but that individual would never advance beyond a local beat patrol officer.

Being a local beat cop in one of the larger cities did not sound all that bad to Robert. But, he had a greater vision for himself. He wanted to be involved in real criminal investigative work.

It was simple in his mind, he would just save his money for college. The problem was that his deputy pay in Janesville did not amount to much. He was able to provide for himself, but he was still living at home. Even with the least amount of living expense, there was little left to save for a college education.

After visiting the police department in Milwaukee, a department considered as exemplary and recognized both nationally and locally, Robert made the decision to accept a job as a patrol officer there. He managed to obtain a small clean room at a boarding house not far from the precinct he would be working out of. Even with the cost of living, the pay as a police officer meant he could save a little more than he had been able to save in Janesville.

In 1904, Robert was hired in at the Milwaukee Police Department under Chief John Janssen. Chief Janssen's appoint-

ment in 1888 marked the end of the old spoils system that re-
warded political cronies with jobs. He became known as "The
Czar," both by the criminals and by his own men, for his strict
enforcement of the law and the Milwaukee Police Department
rules. Janssen was a fearless officer and a strict disciplinarian.
These were the traits that Robert wanted to emulate. He was
looking forward to learning all he could in the department under the direction of this man.

Several years went by, and Robert had performed his duties in an exemplary manner, working long hours every day.
The residents of the neighborhoods he patrolled were mostly
families of German immigrants, and he got along well with
them. His captain praised him and told Robert he should consider going to college as soon as he could.

A few more years went by before Robert had saved enough
to begin college. He would have to work while attending
school, but he knew he was disciplined enough to maintain his
classwork while holding down a part-time job.

After working his way through college, he completed his
degree in criminal justice at the University of Michigan in Ann
Arbor. He secured a position with the Chicago Police Department in 1912. Mature, disciplined, and level-headed, Robert
moved quickly up the ranks achieving detective status earlier
than most others before him.

When the United States entered the Great War in 1917,
Robert joined the United States Army's military police force.
The paramount mission of the military police units was to ad-
minister the selective service law. In the first year of his service, Robert provided standard police style activities in the
United States. His experience on the police force in Chicago
served him well in handling every situation.

In 1918, General Pershing received permission to organize
military police units for support in Europe. Robert became a
member of the Military Police Division and served on the front
lines in France. While these units continued to provide police

activities, Robert's battalion was also responsible for traffic control and security.

The company to which Robert was deployed remained in the rear to clean up after the rest of the units had moved on. There was fierce combat as they battled the enemy stragglers who refused to give up. The military police company was often engaged in heated skirmishes. Once they had the area secured, they were then responsible for handling the prisoners of war.

It was difficult and dangerous work, but Robert performed his duties with valor. He earned a wound chevron after being shot in his side during the Second Battle of Marne in August 1918.

Robert returned to Chicago after the war where he joined the Federal Bureau of Investigation in 1919. His previous experience on the Chicago Police Department and his service in the war aided his entry into the Special Agent program in spite of his age, now just past thirty-six years.

After completing the intense training program in Chicago, Robert was assigned to the Milwaukee FBI office in 1920, now Special Agent Robert Johnson.

Chapter 9

La Porte, 1922.

After the World War, Carl became a naturalized citizen of the United States in 1922. He was quite proud of the accomplishment and expected at least some bit of acknowledgment from Anna. She, however, was only interested in gathering with others for a party after the citizenship ceremony. Later, when she felt that the party was too quiet, she left and went to a local speakeasy to join her friends.

For a few years after the World War ended in 1918, Carl and Anna made an effort to have a closer relationship. But it was not long before Anna again pulled away from her life at home. Carl grew quieter and became despondent, and he looked for comfort deeper in the bottle.

While he still loved his daughters, he no longer felt the joy he had once felt with them. His mother-in-law lived with them now, and she had taken on full responsibility for the children. While she looked down on Carl for his drinking and lack of fatherhood, she truly despised her own daughter and rarely spoke with her.

After the war effort wound down, Advance-Rumely was forced to make cuts in its labor force. Business was still good, but it was not as good as it had grown to be during the war. By the time he had become a citizen, Carl was once again concerned about his employment with the company.

Carl felt like the bottom was about to drop out when he was called to the manager's office in the midst of the large number of job losses. He had seen many men, some he had worked with for ten years, leave the office with lowered heads as they were escorted out of the building. Carl longed for a drink. His hands were shaking as he turned the doorknob and entered the office.

"Carl, please, sit down," the manger said as he motioned to the chair in front of his imposing desk.

Carl noted the large stack of files on the manager's desk. He also noticed that the man's sleeves were rolled up, and his tie was loosened. It was unusual to see him like this. Carl slowly took a seat in the chair.

The manager had taken his position with the company when they merged the Advance and Rumely companies. Carl had not seen much of him in the factory. He seemed to be there only when there was some sort of problem that he felt he could resolve by screaming loudly at one of the workers.

"Carl, I see by our records that you've been with us for twelve years."

"Yessir."

"You started as a blacksmith at the Rumely Company, and you continue to be in that same position."

"Well, yessir, but I've been working with the product development group on new products. That is, I've been more than just a blacksmith." Carl felt as if he had said too much. But then, *Why does it matter if I'm getting fired?*

"Yes, I see." The manager was very matter-of-fact in his tone.

Carl stirred in the chair, and his dry throat wanted a drink very badly.

"You were a very good blacksmith I'm told. But, as you know, we don't have as much need for blacksmiths with the mechanization now deployed in the factory." He stared at the folder of papers in his hands only peering over his glasses briefly as he spoke.

Why doesn't he just get this over with?! Carl fidgeted all the more. He felt sweat forming on his brow.

"Carl, your skills as a blacksmith are useful on occasion with the product group, but . . ."

I know! Just get this over with and fire me!

". . . your abilities to visualize solutions and develop them into working prototypes are exceptional." He lifted his head this time rather than just peering over his glasses.

Carl was dumbfounded. *Why is he praising me when he's about to fire me?*

"Carl, we want to promote you to a full prototype development position. You'll still do some blacksmith work as needed, but we want to give you broader control in our development group. We'll be providing some advanced engineering training for you as well."

Am I hearing him right? "A promotion?" Carl questioned dumbfoundedly

"Yes, Carl. Everyone in the department greatly admires your skills." He paused momentarily and almost appeared to smile. "I understand you're still fondly referred to as The Blacksmith. We know your skills are much broader than that, and you've demonstrated that. Carl, welcome to your new position. Oh, and by the way, there's a pay raise involved as well." The manager reached his hand out to Carl.

With a prideful smile on his face, Carl stood and shook the man's hand. "Thank-you, sir. I'm very much appreciative of this, and I won't let you down."

"Well, see that you don't."

The way the manager said this left Carl unsure if it was a pleasantry or a direct challenge. But, at this point, it didn't matter. Carl wasn't losing his job, he was getting a new job and a raise in pay!

"The group you'll be with will be reporting to Superintendent Herrington. You'll no longer be in the Manufacturing Division. My best to you in your new role, Carl." They released their handshake.

Carl turned to exit the office, "Thank you again, sir."

After work, Carl went to the nearby restaurant with the speakeasy in the backroom with a group of old friends. They were aware of his promotion, and all slapped his back, shook his hand, and wished him well.

Carl ordered a round of drinks for all of them. There were cheers and laughter. But, Carl was looking around to see if Anna was working.

The place was filled with many workers and the few locals who came for dinner. Carl scanned the room for Anna, but he did not see her. He was sure she should be here, so he approached the bartender and asked about Anna.

"Nope, Carl, haven't seen her tonight. I think she's coming in tomorrow."

Several of the men grabbed Carl by the shoulders and led him back to the group. Drinks continued to flow freely throughout the night. Carl eventually removed Anna from his thoughts and enjoyed the drink.

The next day, Carl informed Anna of his promotion at work. She perked up when Carl told her there would be an increase in his pay.

"Carl, we should celebrate. Let's go dancing! Oh, I know, let's go to that nice nightclub out by the lake! Everyone will see us!" She was excited and demanding at the same time.

Carl did not really enjoy going out dancing, and he did not feel comfortable going to a fancy club. "I don't know, Anna," he paused trying to think of an excuse. "Your mother will have to watch the girls all day and all night." He knew it was not a real excuse, as Anna's mother took care of the girls most of the time anyway.

"Carl, don't use my mother as an excuse! If you don't want to go, just say so! But, I am going out tonight to celebrate! Come along if you want." Anna stomped out of the room as Carl stood speechless.

It was no different than most conversations between them. But, Carl wanted things to work. He called after Anna, "Fine, Anna, let's go out tonight . . . together."

Dismally from the other room, "Sure, Carl."

Things were better between Carl and Anna for the next few weeks. Slowly, however, the situation returned to what had become their normal. They were living two separate lives, and Anna had even less desire for her life with Carl, or with her own children.

Carl spent more time at work, partly out of necessity with his new job and partly because he simply did not want to go home. Working longer hours, Carl now seldom met his old friends at the speakeasy.

The group of engineers he now worked with were not the type of men to go out for a drink after work. Carl found himself drawn away from his old friends and mostly drinking alone at a smaller speakeasy not far from his home.

One evening, he was out of work at an early enough time that he thought he might be able to catch up with some of his old friends at the brewpub. Carl popped in and quickly scanned the room searching for his old companions.

He spotted the men, and his eyes met with those of his friend Paul. Paul, however, quickly averted his eyes and spoke to the group seated at a large table. Carl slowly crossed the room toward the table, but as he did, the men scattered from the table, some of them exiting the establishment altogether.

Carl was able to catch up with Paul. "Hey, Paul, what's going on?" He waved his hand at Paul.

Paul looked away for a moment, but he had nowhere to go as Carl approached. "Oh, hi, Carl," he spoke quietly. He looked around to see if the other men were watching him.

"Hey, what's going on? Seems like all the fellas suddenly had to leave."

"Yeah, Carl." He looked down at his drink, then raised it and swallowed the remainder of the glass. "Look, Carl, I have to get going."

Carl caught the man by the shoulder as he prepared to leave. As he did so, the man scowled at Carl. "Carl, you don't want to do that."

Carl felt the threatening tone. "Sorry, Paul. What is it?"

"Look, Carl, you've become too good for the rest of us. You work with the fancy engineers now, and they say you're even going out to that classy club by the lake." He continued scowling at Carl. "I guess you're just too good for your old friends now. I have to go, Carl. I don't need to be keeping company with you."

As the man turned to leave, Carl again grabbed his shoulder. "But, Paul . . ."

Paul turned and threw his fist striking Carl on the jaw. Carl stumbled back into several other men who broke his fall while drinks spilled.

"Stick to your own, Carl!" Paul stomped across the room and pushed the front door violently as he left the bar.

Carl knew better than to pursue Paul. He straightened himself up and stretched his jaw. He found a small table in the corner and sat down. It wasn't long before he had a drink in his hand.

Carl was trying to make sense of what had happened. *Do they really feel that way? I never did anything to make them think I was better than them. I've just had to work differently now. They just don't understand.*

Carl ordered a bottle and remained in the corner until closing time.

He awoke in the morning to a quiet house. It was his day off, but no one else seemed to be around. Carl rose slowly and made himself some breakfast. A short time later, his mother-in-law entered the front door with the girls.

"Where have you been so early with the girls?"

"Carl, Anna has left." She held the girls close to her.

"Left? Where? Does she have to work this early? She never goes in this early." Carl was confused.

"No, Carl, she's gone. She's moved out, and she left the girls with me."

Chapter 10

La Porte, 1926-1933.

Any hope of continuing their marriage had ended years ago. Anna had initially moved into an apartment with some other women, but eventually she took up with a slick Italian who tended bar and ran a gambling game.

There were now only three things in Carl's life: his whiskey, his work, and his children . . . in that order. That was the balance in his life. This was now his normal.

A year ago, Anna filed for a divorce saying that Carl was not providing for her as a wife. Carl no longer cared what she said or thought. The divorce was quickly finalized, and Anna gave Carl full custody of their three daughters now ages thirteen, twelve, and eight. Anna wanted nothing of her life with Carl.

Work continued well for Carl in spite of the loss of Anna and his continued drinking. He was late some mornings, but he was performing in a manner that kept him in high demand. The Blacksmith continued to utilize his skills in the development of new products for Advance-Rumely. He was a member of a highly respected work group. Their work was often done with utmost confidentiality as manufacturers were always trying to gain an edge over one another.

The financial collapse that began in 1929 continued into 1930 and began to weigh heavily on Advance-Rumely. Early in 1930, the company started seeking a buyer. Times were difficult as many employees had their hours cut or were laid off from their jobs. Fortunately, Carl was still working full-time in his role in engineering and development. However, even Carl noticed the decreased interest in new product development at the company.

In May of 1931, the Allis-Chalmers Manufacturing Company, a manufacturer of industrial machinery and farm equipment headquartered in Milwaukee, Wisconsin, completed a buy-out of Advance-Rumely. With overlaps in their tractor lines, the Advance-Rumely tractors were discontinued. Allis-Chalmers was more interested in Advance-Rumely's line of threshing and harvesting machines. They also saw the enormous advanced manufacturing plants that occupied about 80 acres in La Porte as a key advantage for the company. But the greatest attraction to the purchase of Advance-Rumely was its extensive dealership network. These dealerships were almost immediately converted to the complete line of Allis-Chalmers products.

The buy-out and immediate discontinuation of the Advance-Rumely tractor line was a shock to most employees. However, Allis-Chalmers wanted to continue to develop the harvester line of farm machinery at the extensive La Porte plant.

While there were some job lay-offs, product innovation increased after the buy-out by Allis-Chalmers, and Carl became further secure in his position as part of the product development group. He was held in such high regard, that some of the men did what they could to cover for his obvious drinking problem.

That same year, 1931, Carl's two oldest daughters, Marie and Rose, married and left his home. Fourteen-year-old Leona was still in school, and Carl's mother-in-law continued to take care of Leona and the house. Carl thought it odd that he was now getting along quite well with the mother of his former wife.

As with so many others, the bottom dropped out for Carl as the Great Depression worsened throughout the 1930s. He still had his position, but he had been cut back to three eight-hour days per week. The cut in his pay was huge for Carl.

Because of the reduction in his income, Carl did not spend as much time in the local speakeasies. Instead, he brought his bottles of whiskey home, and, on his days off work, he spent most of his time drinking. He isolated himself more and more, ignoring his daughter and mother-in-law, and wallowing in self-pity. It was fortunate that his mother-in-law was around to cook the meager meals the three of them shared.

One afternoon, Carl stopped at a local speakeasy to purchase a bottle of whiskey. He had already been drinking most of the day, and when he found his bottle empty, he immediately left the house.

He staggered into the nearby speakeasy and made his way to the bar. "Hey, Joe, give me a bottle of whiskey."

"Your regular, Carl?"

"Yeah." Carl ordered the cheapest bottle the bar sold.

He looked around and noticed Anna sitting with three men at a table. When Anna saw Carl, she seemed to come to life and flaunt the good time she was having with the men. She was being especially playful with one of the men and pulled him closer to her.

The bartender returned, "Here's your bottle, Carl."

"Thanks." Carl counted out the coins that he had tightly grasped in his fist, placed them on the counter, and turned to leave.

"Wait a minute, Carl! You owe me another two-bits." The man was gruff with Carl.

Carl turned back to the man, muttered something under his breath, and slapped a quarter on the bar top. "Geez, Joe, its not like I'm trying to cheat ya! Take your damn two-bits!"

Carl glanced over at Anna. When she saw him, she looked straight into his eyes, then bent over and kissed the man next to her. It was too much for Carl. He headed directly to the table, albeit a bit unsteadily.

"You, uh, gentlemen, you do know this is a married woman don't you?" Carl stood motionless at the table. He had heard she had married the Italian, but he wasn't really sure.

"What's it to ya, buddy?" said the man nearest Carl. "Get along."

Carl reached out and grabbed the man's shoulder. The man immediately stood and threw a right hook into the side of Carl's face. It was an awkward punch that merely knocked Carl to the side. He stumbled to catch himself and dropped his bottle to the floor.

As Carl looked for the bottle, the man came forward. This time with full force, he hit Carl squarely on the jaw. Carl went down to the floor as the man stood over him and laughed. Slowly and awkwardly, Carl stood ready to face the man.

"I told ya, buddy, to mind your own business and move along." He stared coldly into Carl's eyes.

Carl put his head down and rammed into the man's chest grabbing him and trying to wrestle him to the floor. The man was too strong for Carl, and he tossed Carl to the side. He went after Carl with a fury, throwing blow after blow to Carl's face. Carl barely made any defense and could not make contact with his weak attempts to punch back.

After a blow to Carl's stomach, the man threw an upper cut to Carl's chin that sent him flying backwards into the bar stools. Carl slumped to the floor, his face bloodied.

"Now, get out of here, you drunken bum!" The man lifted Carl from the floor, turned him, and threw a final punch that sent Carl reeling toward the door. Hitting the floor, Carl raised his hand to indicate that he had had enough.

He looked around and saw Anna laughing with the men. His thoughts quickly turned to his bottle of whiskey. He looked around and saw it not far from where he lay. He grabbed a nearby chair to help himself up. He looked down at the bottle and moved slowly toward it. He fumbled with the bottle, but he was able to grasp it. He made straight for the door and left the bar and the laughter behind.

When Carl returned home, his mother-in-law left the room as soon as she saw him. It was not the first time Carl had come home in that condition. She knew better than to even attempt to have a conversation with Carl.

Leona approached her father, "Daddy, sit down. Let me clean you up." She helped him into the chair.

As Leona went into the kitchen, Carl opened his bottle and took a long draft of the fiery liquid. Leona returned with a pan of water and wash rag. "Let me wipe your face, Daddy."

Carl submitted to her attention without saying a word. Leona gently wiped Carl's bloodied face, and Carl simply stared straight ahead. He loved his daughter and appreciated what she did for him, but he could never express himself well to the girls. He was closer to Leona than to the two older girls, and she did more for him than the other two did. In spite of the way Carl treated – or ignored – the family, Leona loved her father.

Chapter 11.

Berlin, Germany, 1933.

In America, the depression was reaching an all-time low with continued bank failures and business closures. In La Porte, Carl was still working three shortened days a week, barely providing for himself, his daughter, and his mother-in-law.

On January 30, 1933, Adolph Hitler was appointed Chancellor of Germany by the President of Germany, Paul von Hindenburg. After previous failed attempts to win the vote, Hitler and the National Socialist German Workers Party (NSDAP) had taken over the country.

One month later, on February 27, the German Parliament building, the Reichstag, was mysteriously set afire and burned to the ground. The new Chancellor immediately issued the Reichstag Fire Decree abolishing German civil liberties.

About another month went by, and hundreds of citizens were arrested as Hitler's National Socialist Party, or Nazi Party as it was known, rounded up their political opponents.

Hitler's emergence marked a crucial turning point for Germany and, ultimately, for the world. His plan, embraced by much of the German population, was to do away with politics and make Germany a powerful, unified one-party state.

Hitler immediately ordered a rapid expansion of the state police, the Gestapo, and put Hermann Goering in charge of a new security force, composed entirely of Nazi Party members dedicated to stamping out whatever opposition to his party might arise. From that moment on, Nazi Germany was off and running, and there was little anyone could do to stop it.

On March 22, the Reichstag passed the Enabling Act, a law that gave Adolf Hitler dictatorial powers. Hitler could now issue decrees independently of the Reichstag and the presidency. It gave Hitler a base from which to carry out the first steps of his National Socialist revolution.

A former German who had immigrated to America and later returned to Germany was one of those who had helped bring Hitler to power. Wilhelm Gegner had grown up in the slums on the streets of east Berlin. The family's residence consisted of two small, crowded rooms for the family with four children. The building, like many of the tenements, was drafty in the winter, sweltering in the summer, and always noisy. For as long as he could remember, Wilhelm knew he would leave the place at his earliest opportunity.

It was more than just the living conditions, however, that led to his desire to abandon the life he knew. Wilhelm's father was a drunk who beat his wife and his children, most often for no reason. Wilhelm longed to be big enough to fight back, whether for himself, his mother, or his siblings.

Wilhelm's father was a shoemaker like his father before him. And, like their father, Wilhelm and his brother Gunther were forced to work for the shoemaker at a very young age. The work was not easy for the boys, and they were regularly berated and beaten for not working fast enough or not performing to their father's meager standards.

For his part, the father was a hardened task master who drank to excess while shouting orders at the boys. His demeanor with the boys was no better with those who came to his business for shoe repairs. Seldom did anyone come to purchase new shoes. The quality of his father's work was poor, since he relied mostly on the efforts of the children. For minimal shoe repair, however, his prices were cheap, and the children could perform the repair work satisfactorily.

The economy in Germany was in poor shape at this time. The worldwide depression that had begun before Wilhelm was even born continued to devastate many businesses. Wilhelm knew, even at his young age, that his father was, and always would be, a miserable failure.

At the age of twelve, Wilhelm left his family and lived on the streets of Berlin with other outcast young boys. He learned to become self-sufficient and strong, surviving on his own. He quickly expanded from panhandling on the streets to petty theft. He organized a small group of other lost youth who looked up to Wilhelm as a leader of their small band of thieves. Wilhelm commanded a degree of respect from the others that fed his ego and encouraged his errant behavior.

He became less tolerant of those who did not show a respect for him, and he developed a callous attitude that eventually turned to savage behavior. He was not above challenging anyone, regardless of age or size. The loser paid a dear price and, in the end, became a follower of Wilhelm. He was feared by the others, and he enjoyed being in that position.

He grew in size and stature on the streets where he ate better than he had ever eaten at home. He was tall with a broad build and strong, large hands like those of his father. He was a good looking young man with straight light brown hair and blue-gray eyes. He had a commanding personality that easily attracted others to him, but he could also intimidate anyone who even thought about defying him, which, of course, no one did.

Hearing of the opportunities in America, Wilhelm laid plans to leave Germany. He learned all he could of the American culture and began to learn the language. Wilhelm was an intelligent young man and had no problem studying the American vocabulary. In a short time, he was teaching his followers the language. This helped him become even more proficient in the subtle wordings and jargon of the English language.

At the age of sixteen, Wilhelm left Germany and made his way to America. There he learned how gangs operated on the mean streets of New York. He learned to speak the language even more fluently and easily folded in as an American. It wasn't long before he was running with some of the toughest young criminals in New York's east side neighborhoods.

Wilhelm could handle himself well in a brawl, and he quickly learned how to fight deftly with a knife. He was remorseless with anyone who crossed him.

Over the years, Wilhelm became a leader in his own right and controlled a sizable neighborhood in New York. He learned the finer art of leadership and control in a business-like manner. He was well-suited for his role in that environment with his antisocial attitude and simple lack of conscience.

While in America, Wilhelm continued to follow the political landscape of Germany. He maintained communications with some of his former gangster friends who had risen to their own level of influence and control. They were supporting Hitler, who used the economic turmoil of the early 1920s to fashion an alliance of right-wing groups and attempt a government coup in November 1923.

As the economy collapsed, the criminal element and their organizations did well for themselves in black market operations. The coup attempt failed as the government reformed the currency and rescheduled war reparation payments to the Allies. It was these and other measures that allowed the economy to recover in 1924.

Encouraged by his German compatriots and assured by the economic turn-around, Wilhelm returned to Berlin in 1926. Rising quickly in the criminal element, Wilhelm was seen as an intelligent, mature, and ruthless leader.

One of the first things he discovered upon returning to Germany was Adolph Hitler's book, *Mein Kampf*. After reading the book, Wilhelm realized he wanted to be part of something that he saw as a grand opportunity. He openly supported the NSDAP voting for the party in 1928, unfortunately for him, being one of fewer than three percent of the population who did so. But as events unfolded in 1933, Hitler was elected Chancellor of Germany, and Wilhelm had helped elect him.

1933 brought about many other significant changes in Germany. In April, a law was passed forcing all non-Aryans to retire from the legal profession and civil service positions. Also in April, Jewish kosher rituals for the killing of animals was outlawed. In May, the Nazis staged massive public book burnings throughout Germany. In July, all non-Nazi parties were outlawed, and the formation of new political parties was forbidden. It was only the beginning of the horrors yet to come.

Chapter 12

Akron, Ohio, 1935.

Prohibition officially ended with the repeal of the Eighteenth Amendment to the U.S. Constitution in 1933. It was never illegal to drink during Prohibition. The Eighteenth Amendment and the Volstead Act never barred the consumption of alcohol, just making it, selling it, and shipping it for mass production and consumption.

Hotels and restaurants looked joyously forward to what they hoped would be a new boom in business. There was some concern among hotel keepers, however, that the liquor regulations would prohibit sales of hard liquor by the glass, thus preventing a return of the popular hotel bar.

In La Porte, the speakeasies were opened anew for business. Some of the smaller speakeasies that had popped up closed nearly as quickly as they had opened. Speakeasies were gone, and taverns were now open. Guenther's brewpub was officially back in business. Carl was caught up with a number of others in celebrating the freedom to drink again. Best of all, the economy was improving slightly over the previous two years.

In Akron, Ohio, Dr. Robert H. Smith, Dr. Bob as he was known, a surgeon, eased his way back into his old beer drinking habit. However, it wasn't long before he was drinking over a case of beer a day, further braced with hard liquor. He was a hopeless alcoholic.

Early in his medical career, he recognized his drinking problem. In ensuing years, Dr. Bob checked himself into more than a dozen hospitals and sanitariums in an effort to stop his drinking. The passage of Prohibition in 1919 had encouraged him, but he soon discovered that the exemption for medicinal alcohol, and bootleggers, could supply more than enough to continue his excessive drinking.

For the next seventeen years, his life revolved around how to subvert his wife's efforts to stop his drinking and obtain the alcohol he craved while trying to hold together a medical practice in order to support his family . . . and his drinking.

Dr. Bob's wife had attended a lecture by the founder of an organization known as the Oxford Group. Its appeal was in the application of certain principles in daily living, namely honesty, purity, unselfishness, and love. Oxford Groupers, as they were called, had success with those trying to stop drinking.

For the next two years, Dr. Bob and his wife attended local meetings of the group in an effort to solve his alcoholism. Dr. Bob's membership at Akron had not helped him enough to achieve sobriety, however. He was having difficulty with the spiritual aspect, as in his youth his parents took him to religious services four times a week, and, in response, he determined he would never attend religious services when he grew up.

In New York, William G. Wilson had been a golden boy on Wall Street, enjoying success and power as a stockbroker. But, he was literally drinking himself to death. Bill's wife, with the help of her brother-in-law, a doctor, was able to have him admitted to Towns Hospital in New York. Bill was subjected to the "belladonna cure" which involved "purging and puking" aided by castor oil. Belladonna, a hallucinogen, was used to ease the symptoms of alcohol withdrawal.

In July of 1934, Bill was admitted to Towns Hospital for a second time. There, psychiatrist William D. Silkworth explained to Bill that alcoholism was a physical allergy to alcohol and not a moral malady. This allergy, the doctor said, was triggered by consumption of even a small amount of alcohol that caused a compulsion to drink along with a mental obsession to do so in some people.

Unfortunately, almost immediately upon his discharge, Bill started drinking again. He was unemployable, deep in debt, suicidal, and drinking around the clock.

By September, Bill was admitted for the third time. This time, his doctor pronounced Bill as hopeless and informed his wife that Bill would likely have to be committed. Bill left the hospital a broken man, and only sheer terror kept him sober.

In December 1934, after drinking four beers on the way, Bill admitted himself to the Towns Hospital. A visitor told Bill about the principles of an organization known as the Oxford Group. When his visitor left, Bill fell into a deep depression and had a profound spiritual experience after crying out, "If there be a God, will he show himself?!"

Fearing that he had gone crazy, Bill called for his doctor who told him to hang on to what he had experienced because it seemed so much better than what he came into the hospital with. Bill had undergone a powerful spiritual experience unlike anything he had ever known. His depression and despair were lifted, and he felt free and at peace.

The Oxford Groups in America were headed by the noted Episcopal clergyman, Dr. Samuel Shoemaker. Under this spiritual influence, and with the help of an old friend, Bill had gotten sober and had then maintained his recovery by working with other alcoholics.

Six months into his own sobriety, Bill and a couple of friends located a small company in Akron, Ohio, that was ripe for takeover and would pull Bill and his wife out of the severe financial situation they were in. Unfortunately, the deal collapsed due to stories of Bill's drinking, and Bill, dejected and distressed, returned to his hotel where he nearly drank again.

Tempted by the lure of the bar, Bill headed to the public phone booth instead and desperately sought another alcoholic, someone like himself, to talk to. He contacted the leader of the local Oxford Group who gave him a list of ten names. After a series of calls, Bill eventually contacted Dr. Robert H. Smith, who he discovered was an Akron surgeon and some-time attendee at Oxford Group meetings.

Agreeing to the meeting only to appease his wife, Dr. Bob was determined to spend no more than fifteen minutes with this man who claimed to have a cure for alcoholism. The two found in one another, however, kindred spirits united by the common bond of alcoholism. Bill needed help to keep from drinking; Dr. Bob needed help to stop. The two men went into a room for what Bob thought would be a quick talk, but he was mistaken. For Dr. Bob, this was the first living human with whom he had ever talked who knew what he was talking about with regard to alcoholism from actual experience.

Bill emphasized that alcoholism was a malady of the mind, the emotions, and the body. This was the all-important fact that he had learned from Dr. Silkworth at Towns Hospital. Though a physician, Dr. Bob had not known alcoholism to be a disease. They finally concluded their intense discussion about five hours later.

Dr. Bob drank once again a couple of weeks later after coming home from a medical conference in New Jersey. But Dr. Bob took his last drink June 10, 1935 – the founding date of Alcoholics Anonymous, the day there were two sober people in fellowship, and the day Dr. Bob drank for the last time.

The two men worked together reaching out to alcoholics in Dr. Bob's hometown of Akron, Ohio, through the summer of 1935. Two guiding principles were born in that summer. First, an alcoholic needed another alcoholic to work with him, and, secondly, the alcoholic must live a one-day-at-a-time philoso-phy. By the end of the year, they had a small fellowship of two groups in New York and Akron.

Chapter 13

Berlin, Germany, 1936-1938.

Under the Treaty of Versailles, signed in 1919 after the Great War, Germany was prohibited from forming any type of military intelligence organization. Despite this prohibition, in 1920 Germany formed an espionage group within the Ministry of Defense. The initial purpose of the *Abwehr*, as it was known, was defense against foreign espionage targeting Germany. The *Abwehr* was not initially a foreign intelligence gathering organization – its stated objective was to protect Germany from foreign intruders.

The *Abwehr* did not have a good relationship with the growing paramilitary group known as the *SS* under Adolph Hitler and the National Socialist German Workers Party, abbreviated as the Nazi Party. The Nazi *SS*, or *Schutzstaffel* (Protection Squadron), was making its power felt as the foremost agency of security, surveillance, and terror within Germany.

When the Nazi Party came to power under the leadership of Hitler, the *SS* came to be considered a state organization and a branch of the government. Law enforcement gradually came under control of the *SS*, and many *SS* organizations became actual government agencies. The *SS* established a police state within the German government, using the secret state police and security forces to suppress resistance to Hitler.

The strength of the *SS* only increased the animosity between it and the *Abwehr*. The *Abwehr* began to covertly undermine the very regime under which they served. Members of the *Abwehr* were torn, to some degree, over loyalty, but more so over the fear of the *SS* organization.

It was within this framework that the thug Wilhelm Gegner continued his stronghold of power on the streets of Berlin. Now in his early fifties, he was too old to even think he could join the *SS*. But, on the inside of the larger organization, he could see himself wielding power over others and growing in strength and influence. As such, Wilhelm had eagerly joined Hitler's German Workers Party in 1928.

Wilhelm's awareness of the situation and his ability to find an alternate plan to be in a position of strength led to his decision to pursue a role within the *Abwehr*. He was aware that his mastery of the English language was a great advantage for him to such an organization. His talent to manipulate others and steer them in his desired direction would help him secure a place of importance. He felt confident about his plans.

The *Abwehr* was reorganized within the Hitler regime. Under new leadership, its numbers increased dramatically from fewer than 150 members to nearly one-thousand members between 1935 and 1937. By 1938, the *Abwehr* was divided into three main sections:

First was the Central Division which acted as the control point for the other two sections, as well as handling personnel and financial matters, including the payment of agents.

Next was the Foreign Branch, which had several functions including evaluation of captured documents and evaluation of foreign press and radio broadcasts.

Abwehr itself became the third division and focused on intelligence gathering. It was subdivided into many areas of responsibility including foreign intelligence gathering, falsification of documents, communications, and economic intelligence. *Abwehr* frequently disguised its organization by attaching its personnel to the German Embassy or to trade missions.

The *Abwehr* was fairly active and effective as it built a wide range of contacts. There was even some significant penetration into the United States with regard to its industrial capacity and economic potential. *Abwehr* also collected data concerning American military capabilities and contingency planning.

After assuming absolute control over all intelligence activities in 1938, Hitler declared that he did not want men of intelligence under his command, but men of brutality. Working within this organization was a perfect fit for Wilhelm.

It became increasingly important for Germany to obtain intelligence on equipment being sent to Great Britain, data on Atlantic shipping, and the general war potential of the United States. Much of this was readily available from the press and other open sources in the United States to German diplomatic personnel. However, to supplement these sources and evade British censorship, the *Abwehr* established espionage networks which relayed information from the United States to Germany by radio and other clandestine communications methods.

Through his gift for self-promotion, his willingness to use bribery, and his ruthless disregard for convention, Wilhelm Gegner was able to place himself in a favorable light to key personnel in the Central Division. He exposed them to his specific capabilities with conviction assuring that they could not deny that he would be an asset to the organization.

By the end of 1938, Wilhelm Gegner was recruited into the *Abwehr* where he began his training to be a foreign spy for deployment to the United States of America.

Chapter 14

Milwaukee, 1938-1939.

With the events unfolding in Germany throughout 1938, the United States Department of War had begun top secret talks evaluating scenarios surrounding Germany's aggression toward other countries under the direction of German Chancellor Adolf Hitler. One commission was assigned to determine what type of support the United States would provide to Great Britain and other nations allied against Germany.

This group determined that it would take a large effort by U.S. manufacturing to retool their factories to support production of military vehicles, and not just transport vehicles, but battlefield vehicles including armored tracked vehicles and tanks.

Tank design had undergone many changes since the Great War. The War Department became focused on lighter tanks that would support infantry troops in field operations. The official doctrine of the War Department was that tanks were employed to assist the advance of infantry foot troops, either preceding or accompanying the infantry assault echelon. These tanks, intended specifically for infantry support, would take out enemy emplacements and infantry concentrations.

But, with intelligence gathered on Germany's growing military forces, there was a body within the War Department that felt the U.S. should be preparing a modern design of the tank with a single purpose – to destroy the well-armored tanks of the German military.

This new tank would need to meet strict specifications under some guiding principles. First was mechanical reliability. The vehicles had to operate longer with fewer repair parts. Secondly, the size of these tanks must be compatible with field bridging equipment, thus restricting the width and realizing a maximum weight of thirty tons. Third, speed was of utmost importance. The tank must be able to run at least twenty-five miles per hour in the field and forty-five miles per hour on roads. And finally, the tanks must mount a 75mm cannon capable of destroying an enemy tank. To this end, the emerging anti-tank gun designs were already being modified to fit tanks. These weapons fired smaller shells, but at higher velocities with higher accuracy, improving their performance against armor.

Top secret meetings were set up with every major vehicle manufacturer in the United States. The War Department also reached out to agricultural implement manufacturers whose expertise at building powerful track equipped crawler tractors could be directed to tracked vehicles.

It was within the guidance of these constraints that a War Department commission met with Max Babb, president of Allis-Chalmers, the third largest producer of farm equipment, in Milwaukee, Wisconsin. The War Department laid out a grim scenario should the U.S. not provide support for Great Britain and other European countries. The level-headed and strong-willed president was more than willing to work with the War Department on what was now designated as a top secret project.

Further meetings over the next several weeks between the War Department and a select group of the executive team provided the program objectives and complete design specifications to the company. And, after conferring on the needs for secrecy, the decision was made to develop the tank at a location outside of Milwaukee and West Allis. The War Department agreed that an opportunity to develop the project at a location without the high profile of the company headquarters would be preferred. Enemy espionage would be more likely to focus on the headquarters, so a remote location would have one more step of separation to protect it.

A small town in Indiana with a reputation for innovation and quality would serve perfectly. In early 1938, the plant had begun producing a new crawler tractor, Model HD14. It was a larger, heavier version of previous crawler tractor models, and being the most advanced model, it was felt it would be a good platform for the Allis-Chalmers tank design.

President Babb himself would deliver the news to the former Advance-Rumely factory in La Porte, Indiana. The executive team had already determined that this program would initially be very limited in size as far as number of workers for the project. The types of workers required were specifically identified including engineers, product design and development experts, and the best production employees. The program had to be developed from top to bottom with the final product ready for production on a new assembly line. All of this would need to be done in the most secretive manner.

Mr. Babb met with the local La Porte Plant President, Donald Scholl, and Engineering and Development Plant Superintendent, Raymond Herrington. It was clear from the beginning that limited knowledge of the program must be maintained. Anything less than complete secrecy could be interpreted as treason. The men signed papers authorizing the War Department to thoroughly review their backgrounds. The same would be required for every man assigned to the project team. Mr. Babb would leave it to Mr. Scholl and Mr. Herrington to select the best men for the team.

Project Rubber Tire, as it was designated to remain inconspicuous, would be developing the M11-AC Gun Motor Carriage for the United States War Department. The M11-AC was a mobile anti-tank gun, commonly known as a tank destroyer (TD). A 75mm forward facing gun would be mounted in a casement form without a moving turret. This would save weight and provide a more mechanically reliable configuration. It would also save production time and cost.

The War Department wanted a motor capable of achieving the required high speeds for the tank. Allis-Chalmers was given the option to use a new General Motors engine already in early production if they felt the development of a new Allis-Chalmers engine would slow down the overall production of the actual vehicle. Using the General Motors engine was the direction the board of Project Rubber Tire decided to take. While Allis-Chalmers had its own engines, they agreed that the new GM engine would surpass Allis-Chalmers' current engine line.

The new GM 6-71 engine would be available in a twin engine configuration known as the 6046. This would be perfect for their design, providing the speed and power to meet the War Department's specifications. Six such engines were ordered by Allis-Chalmers for the development team. The tight-knit unit could now work on developing the armored vehicle itself based on the Model HD14 chassis.

The real design challenge was developing the armor plating. The problem here was that only a slight addition to the thickness of armor plate greatly increased the total weight of the tank, thereby requiring a more powerful and heavier engine. This, in turn, resulted in a larger and heavier transmission and suspension system. Just this sort of vicious cycle aimed at upgrading a tank's most vital characteristics tended to make the tank less maneuverable, slower, and a larger and easier target.

The engineers were presented with a challenge that resulted in numerous proposed solutions and much disagreement. The engineers were pleased to have a casement design that eliminated a moving turret. This would allow accommodation of the more powerful 75mm anti-tank gun without incurring the additional weight of a turret. The lack of a turret also increased the vehicle's internal volume, allowing for increased ammunition stowage and crew comfort.

Specifications from the War Department indicated that the thickness of the steel armor would need to be between two and three inches in the front of the tank. The minimum thickness in other areas was specified at one-half inch.

Early design estimates showed that using the HD14 chassis with the GM 6046 engine would place the gross weight of the tank at thirty-five to forty tons, well over the thirty-ton design limit. The design and engineering teams went to work fine-tuning the body design to require less surface area while maintaining all of the internal space requirements. Only at the very minimum armor specifications could the team even begin to approach the weight limit.

Carl had not been involved in the early design phase of the tank. He and some of the others were assigned to design some of the basic production line elements. The full building would allow for an accelerated production line. They were able to take advantage of some of the new production line improvements that had already been put in place for the HD14 itself.

When Carl got word of the problems the engineers were having with the weight of the armor, he became interested. He approached Superintendent Herrington about the issue.

After ushering Carl into his office, Mr. Herrington closed the door and showed Carl to the conference table. "Carl, as I know you're aware, we must be cautious when discussing Rubber Tire."

"Yes, I know, Mr. Herrington. But I wanted to talk to you about an issue we're facing with the weight of the armor plating. With my experience in metallurgy and problem solving, I'd sure like to look into some of the issues I hear the engineers are facing. I have some ideas that I think might help."

Mr. Herrington changed the subject. "Carl, how are you coming with the production line?"

"Well, sir, we're as far as we can go until we have the final design completed. The chassis build is fully ready, but we need the final design to complete the calibrations of the equipment."

"I see. So, what thoughts are you having?"

"I'd like to look at some options of providing an armor that is not all steel. I have some ideas on using other elements surrounded by steel that could provide the strength while keeping the weight down."

"Carl, you know I appreciate your input, but I feel that the engineers are looking at all the latest developments in armor plating. I'm not sure you would really offer anything they haven't already thought of."

Carl stirred in his chair, seeing that he was not getting his point across. "But, this is a new idea. Something new. I know this will sound a little crazy." Carl was now obviously nervous. He paused searching for his words while Mr. Herrington frowned.

"I mean, well, have they thought about using hardened rubber?" Carl stared at Mr. Herrington looking for a response.

Mr. Herrington appeared momentarily dumbfounded. "Rubber? Carl, these tanks will be facing large shells from opposing tanks! Do you think these shells are going to just bounce off the rubber?" Mr. Herrington laughed.

"Carl, you do realize that Rubber Tire is simply an inconspicuous name for this project, don't you? We aren't designing rubber tanks." He shook his head as he continued to laugh.

Carl had to explain. "You don't understand, sir . . ."

Mr. Herrington interrupted as his laughter stopped and his tone changed, "Carl, I think it's best to leave this to the real engineers. I know you have some good qualifications, Carl, but these are men with college degrees who're working directly with the War Department. No disrespect to you, Carl, but I believe this work is over your head. Time is critical, and we can't be wasting the engineers' time chasing, well, let's just say irresponsible ideas."

Carl wanted to express himself better, but he couldn't seem to come up with better words. Finally, "But, sir, it's a sandwich of rubber between . . ."

Mr. Herrington raised his voice, "Carl! Carl, is your drinking under control? You know we've counted on you to stay focused on your task. Do I need to take some action here?"

Carl was frustrated, and he gave up, "No, sir. I'm fine. Just forget it. I'm sorry to have bothered you."

"Carl, if you need to take a few days off, that can be arranged."

Carl stood and headed for the door. "No, sir, I'm fine."

"One more thing, Carl. You know the importance of secrecy. You cannot be discussing every crazy thought about this project. Don't come to me unless it is of real importance. Are we clear?"

"Yes, sir," Carl sighed.

Back in the plant, Carl didn't know what to do. He knew there was merit to his idea. It was simple really. Between layers of steel armor would be two layers of rubber, one very hard. It was a sandwich which would dissipate the energy of the shell requiring less steel in the armor, thus a lighter weight. He knew it sounded crazy, but in his mind, he had gone through all of the specifics. He had begun to work out the mathematics, but he needed some help with the structural components of the rubber. The steel part was easy for him. He had worked out how much steel could be used in the sandwich. His simplest calculations showed that he could save twenty percent of the weight. This would easily solve the design problem.

Carl stopped at a tavern after work. His frustrations got the better of him, and he had to have a drink. He could not turn off his mind to the problem. While he drank, he found himself making more notes. The key was in the rubber. He needed to determine the ability of the rubber at various hardness levels to distribute the shock wave from the shell.

Unfortunately, because of the nature of Project Rubber Tire, he could not discuss this with anyone outside of the team. He slammed his empty glass down on the table, and left the tavern amid stares.

Chapter 15

La Porte, 1938-1939.

The following morning, Carl awoke still stirred with frustration. He knew he had to talk with one of the engineers. He also knew he would likely face the same response as he did with Mr. Herrington. So, he decided to approach the issue from a different angle.

He needed more information on the rubber component. He could possibly find something in the engineering books at work, but he was not even sure where to begin. But, he had another idea in mind.

Carl arrived at the plant early. He waited just inside the doorway until he saw one of the engineers, John, enter the building. With his head lowered, Carl bumped into John when he entered the building.

Carl looked up, "Oh, sorry, John. I was just trying to figure some things in my head and wasn't paying attention."

"That's okay, Carl." John turned to walk away.

"Hey, John, maybe you could help me." Carl did not wait for John to decline. "I was working on motor mounts for the GM engine . . ."

"Carl, you know we can't discuss this here." John looked around to see if anyone was nearby.

"Oh, yeah. Sorry, John. Can we speak in the plant for a moment?"

"Sure, Carl."

After they passed through security and entered the plant, Carl continued, "Anyway, about the motor mounts for the GM 6046, we've done some small tests on the production line, and I'm not sure the rubber mounts are heavy enough. I hate to burden you guys with this since you have more important issues. So, I was wondering where I might get some information on rubber hardness, structural compositions, and things like that. Maybe I can come up with a quick fix." He hoped he had not spoken too quickly and too eagerly as to arouse suspicion. He waited for John to reply.

"I'll see what I can find, Carl. We have spec sheets on all product components, and I can get you a rubber materials manual that should help. How about I get that to you at lunch?"

"That would be great, John. Thanks. Have a great day!"

By late in the afternoon, Carl had absorbed pages of information on rubber molecular structure and the Shore Hardness Scale. The standard test method, Carl learned, is to press a ball of known size against a piece of rubber with a known force for a given time, and measure how much the rubber "indents" in that time. The deflection gained is then converted into a scale, with lower numbers, such as 40, being soft, and higher numbers, such as 80, being hard.

It was just what he needed. He found out that a rubber tire had a hardness of 70 on the Shore scale. Carl could see the solution in his mind. A shell hitting an outer steel layer would suffer some destruction. It would then enter a rubber layer which would absorb some of the energy as a shock wave was transferred through the softer rubber. A second layer of hardened rubber would absorb additional energy. The final layer of steel would bulge with the energy that was dispersed, but it would resist complete breakdown.

Carl knew it would work, but how could he prove it? He went to work further refining his idea. He worked out the steel requirements based on some assumed rubber reactions. He finally arrived at a design consisting of a one-and-one-half inch outer steel layer, a one inch layer of 70 hardness rubber, a thin steel mesh, an 80 hardness level rubber layer, and a three-quarter inch inner steel layer. The armor would be four and a quarter inches thick while providing the same, or better, protection than the three inch steel armor. Best of all, the weight savings would be about twenty-five percent using two and a quarter inches of steel instead of three inches.

Unfortunately, there was no way for Carl to test his idea. He obviously did not have access to anything close to a 75mm tank shell to fire at a sample. Nor did he have a place to do any test firing.

His brain went to work once again. He could scale his idea down from a 75mm shell to a .30-06 rifle cartridge. The size was easy enough to scale as the .30-06 cartridge was nearly ten percent the diameter of the 75mm shell. As best as Carl could determine, the 75mm round contained about 330 grains of gunpowder, while a .30-06 round contained about 55 grains of powder. By Carl's calculation, the .30-06 would be a bit more powerful than he needed for a ten percent scale comparison, but it would serve as a starting point.

Over the next week, Carl created a two-foot square sample of his steel-and-rubber sandwich. He used thicknesses of ten percent of his specifications. The entire piece was 0.425 inches thick, and the two steel pieces were 0.225 inches thick. He had had the soft rubber made from tire material, while he had a sample of the hard rubber crafted under the guise of the need for new engine mounts. Finally, he made a two-foot square of 0.300-inch steel to represent the three-inch armor.

Carl was able to construct his test samples with no problem. No one questioned what he was working on. Now, the problem was how to test it. He couldn't very well take the armor plates out of the building. And, maybe just as troubling, it would take approval from Mr. Herrington to bring a .30-06 rifle into the building to fire some test rounds.

He had put weeks of focus and effort into his development, but he was once again frustrated. He had not been to the tavern for nearly a week. He felt it was well past time to stop there. He left work right as the factory whistle blew and went for a drink.

As he sat there, he became angry over his situation. He knew what he was doing, but he couldn't get any support. He closed the place down and staggered home, still upset, but not remembering why.

The engineers had arrived at a minimal design using hardened steel that they thought would meet the specifications and come extremely close to meeting the weight requirement. They would leave it up to the design team to take out the additional weight in the design, perhaps in some changes to the chassis.

This was good news for Carl as he found out that they were going to perform tests on the hardened steel design. He inserted himself as best as he could to the point where he was able to take his steel samples out of the building when the engineers were heading to the field to test their hardened steel.

They headed south out of town to an area near Kingsbury that was recently purchased by the War Department. There were rumors regarding the government's use of the 13,000-acre area, but for now, the War Department had given the approval to use a small, remote area for testing.

The engineering team had a much more elaborate set-up for testing than Carl's planned test. They had three samples of their hardened steel to test. Carl had his own thoughts on what would happen. He felt that the steel had been overly hardened to the point of making it brittle. The test on all three samples proved him out. There was disappointment all around, even though there was some expectation that the steel might fail.

Carl stepped up and asked if he could test a sample that he had brought along. The men were surprised at Carl's request, but since they were all gathered there already, they consented. They were a bit put off that Carl would not test in the same manner as they had, but after he explained his process for testing, they again gave their cautious approval.

First, Carl wheeled out his 50-pound 0.300-inch steel sheet and set it up. He then returned to the firing line. Picking up the rifle, he fired the .30-06 round, and it penetrated the steel. No one was surprised.

When they saw Carl's second sample, they all felt it could possibly stop the .30-06 round as it was much thicker. Then Carl had them lift the cart with the sample piece and compare it to the steel he had just penetrated. They were all surprised at the weight difference. They wanted to know how Carl had made the steel so much lighter.

Carl stopped the conversation. "Look, if this works, I'll let you know. If not, I guess I'll have failed."

They looked at Carl with some trust based upon his past innovations. "Carl, if this works, we might agree that you're on to something. Go ahead."

Carl set up his sample and returned to the group. He loaded a round in the rifle, took aim, and fired. The target remained standing, but no holes were visible. They had all heard a hit, but assumed Carl had once again shot the first sample.

"Hey, Carl, nice shot," one of the engineers chided while the others laughed. "Try again and see of you can hit your 'secret' sample."

Carl chambered a second round. He knew he had hit his target with the first round. His heart was now pounding. His second shot hit, and again the target was not penetrated.

This time the men realized that Carl had actually hit the target. They were all stunned. "Carl, what the heck is that?!"

As Carl put the rifle down, they all ran to the target. When they arrived, they looked at the back side. There were two small bulges in the metal, but no holes.

Some of the men still doubted. "Carl, that's nice, but your test isn't really a controlled test. You've merely shown that a rifle bullet didn't penetrate your sample."

"Yeah, Carl, we can't be sure this would really work with this simple test."

Carl spoke up, "Look, I know what you're saying. It's just that I couldn't get Mr. Herrington to even consider my idea. He wouldn't let me approach you guys. I'm ready to turn this over to you to see if this will truly meet the standards of the project."

"Carl, you've proven yourself in the past. I think I speak for all of us when I say . . . yes! We want to take a look at your idea."

They all began throwing questions at Carl about his steel. Carl thought he would burst with pride. *Finally!*

It was only days later when the engineers completed all of their calculations on Carl's sandwich design. They were actually able to improve upon Carl's design making better use of the rubber hardness measurements. They would be able to shave a fraction of an inch off the steel plates saving even more weight, arriving at a twenty-seven percent savings.

A final test conducted by the engineers confirmed the design. They had something that would change the construction of armor forever. Their M11-AC tank would easily weigh in under thirty tons, provide the protection needed on the battlefield, and be able to carry more ammunition or additional troops if needed. The weight savings also meant that the GM 6046 twin engine would easily outperform the speed requirements of the project.

To avoid any issues with Mr. Herrington, Carl asked the engineers to leave his name out of the design. They all wanted Carl to get the credit he deserved, but they agreed to Carl's wishes. However, they made sure to include his name in the patent, even if it did belong to the United States Government - "Carl Schmidt, The Blacksmith."

Chapter 16

Milwaukee, 1939.

Wilhelm Gegner was now part of a cell of German agents under the leadership of veteran Nazi spy Frederick "Fritz"
Duquesne. Their main focus was on industrial plants in America. A shortwave communications network had been set up on
the east coast of the United States with relays to Mexico. The
role of the spies was to discover all they could about U.S. production supporting the European war effort on behalf of the
allied nations lining up against Germany. Of greatest concern
was support that might be under development for Great
Britain.

It was becoming apparent that war would break out soon,
and while the U.S. was officially saying it would stay out of the
war, it was well understood that it would be supporting Great
Britain and the other nations joining them against Germany.
The Hitler regime needed to know what capabilities the U.S.
would be providing. Duquesne himself had already stolen
plans from a plant in Delaware describing a new bomb being
developed in the U.S. This success encouraged more bold
moves in the U.S. by the *Abwehr*.

The highly trained operatives of the Duquesne spy ring
were deployed in various locations in the United States where
key manufacturing was done. This meant that the spies were
positioned not only in the eastern United States, but also
across the Midwestern states. In all, there were thirty-three

members of the Duquesne covert operations team deployed in America by 1939. Their assignments were commensurate with their skills and training.

Wilhelm Gegner's experience in criminal operations provided him with some of the best qualifications for the Duquesne intelligence gathering group. He was a smooth talker who could turn into a ruthless assassin at a moment's notice. He was cool and calm at all times with an engaging personality. He trusted no one but himself, yet he was in complete support of the Hitler regime. While he had developed his skills in the crime world, he was an intelligent man who could readily assess any situation and see an alternate approach when needed.

The *Abwehr's* most recently dispatched agent, Wilhelm was sent to Milwaukee, Wisconsin, the location of the headquarters of the Allis-Chalmers Corporation. With its diverse array of products, Allis-Chalmers had been able to secure major government contracts. The company had provided the giant hydraulic turbines for the Hoover Dam in the mid-1930s. During the Great War, the firm produced engines, gun systems, and electrical controls for aircraft, ships, and tracked vehicles. Currently, it was thought to be ramping up production of similar products for the coming war in Europe.

The corporation's West Allis plant in west Milwaukee employed over 10,000 workers by 1939 and continued to grow. With forged documents, Wilhelm gained access to the plant under the guise of a government accountant. To place an agent in such a position was one of the more daring moves of the spy organization. Wilhelm was heavily scrutinized upon presenting himself to the company, but his forged papers were all in order. His position provided an opportunity to evaluate the degree of Allis-Chalmers' growth in manufacturing in support of Great Britain, as well as any potential for America's entrance into the war.

Many of the German agents had been living in the U.S. for a number of years and had become naturalized citizens. Since

this was not the case for Wilhelm, false records had been prepared to provide complete documentation and a backstory for
his work as a government accountant. He had undergone an
intense training regimen in accounting in preparation for his
role. A quick study, he was able to rapidly establish his skills.

As with many large U.S. manufacturers, Allis-Chalmers'
new role with the military was not uncommon. As such, it was
completely within reason for government accountants to be
assigned within the organization, and, indeed, there were already a number of such individuals in place. Wilhelm would
be nearly invisible within the company's large accounting department.

It was a risky assignment, however, and Wilhelm was given
great leeway in how he would meet the objectives. If his skills
failed him, he would fall back on his charm. If that failed him,
a ruthless resolution would be effortless for him. In fact,
somewhere not deep beneath the surface, he hoped it would
come to just that. He wanted to prove himself to the *Abwehr*
in a big way.

In the U.S., Wilhelm directed his findings to fellow agent
Paul Fehse in New Jersey. His reports were prepared in coded
messages which were then translated by Fehse and transmit-
ted to Germany through Mexico. His correspondence was easily disguised in the form of accounting reports. At this time,
Fehse was Wilhelm's only contact in America.

Wilhelm's reports supported everything that Germany had
expected as they showed a growing production of tractors and
other machinery suitable for use in the war. But, for the most
part, there was nothing unexpected in his findings. The company was performing much like it had during the Great War.

But, then, Wilhelm proved his value when he was able to
determine that there was a direct effort by Allis-Chalmers to
build a new model of an armored battlefield tracked vehicle.
He felt this was a huge disclosure for the Duquesne organization, and, more importantly to his ego, he saw this as a feather
in his cap within the *Abwehr*. His pride was further boosted

when he was directed to take full control over discovery of plans and timelines for this particular piece of war machinery.

Wilhelm knew he could make a real name for himself in *Abwehr*, and beyond, if he could deliver the plans. As he understood it, this new armored vehicle would be unlike anything currently in use. Germany was concerned how its deployment would affect a ground war in Europe. With war imminent, uncovering the plans for the vehicle could be one of the keys to defeating those countries allying themselves against Germany.

Wilhelm dug deeply under the guise of his role as a government accountant. He took great pleasure in duping the unsuspecting Americans to provide him key information. The company's budget and government oversight of the project provided a virtual road map for his efforts.

Many of the company's bookkeepers initially felt like their own work was being watched and questioned by the government man, creating a cautious attitude toward him. Wilhelm, however, quickly charmed many of the workers, especially the women, into actually liking him.

Wilhelm often found himself smiling, and those he was working with began to feel comfortable around him. They did not know that the reason for his smile was the satisfaction he found in so easily gaining their trust and deceiving them. Some of the women found it appealing to see him so carefree as he occasionally chuckled to himself while working.

Wilhelm uncovered the fact that the development of the new armored tank was being done at a remote plant. On the paper trail he followed, the location was only referred to as Project Rubber Tire/Plant R. He knew it was not located in West Allis, but R, perhaps indicating remote, left it wide open as to location.

Everyone he worked with had no idea where Plant R was located. They only knew it was a remote location where Allis-Chalmers was working on a secretive project for the United States military. An important project at Plant R was almost common knowledge, but no one owned up to knowing any details about it.

Wilhelm dug in and worked day and night looking into every remote location determining what products were being developed there or had been developed there in the past. Some locations were easily dismissed as they were engaged in making smaller components like transmissions, steering parts, and electrical systems. These sites would not be set up to develop an entire vehicular system like a field tank.

While the accountants and bookkeepers admired his hard work and long hours, they were also a bit concerned that he might be trying to find something they had done wrong. But, as weeks went by, no negative reports were being produced. In fact, the accountant went out of his way to note the quality and accuracy of their work. He told them how important their contributions were to the overall good of not only the company, but also of the country.

They were softened up to the point where Wilhelm felt he could try to get more information out of them. He focused in on two female supervisors over a large group of bookkeepers in two separate wings of the main office.

His plan was to convince one or both of them to divulge any information that might help him. He warmed up to both of them, sought their assistance, and thanked them profusely for their cooperation. He managed to work in a few lunch breaks with each of the women.

After several more weeks, Wilhelm had narrowed his search down to three locations. There was another plant in Wisconsin, a plant in Missouri, and a plant in Indiana. All three of the plants had manufactured tractors and other types of large farm equipment, including tracked crawlers.

Wilhelm first focused on the La Crosse, Wisconsin, site. It seemed to make the most sense to him since it was located in the same state as the headquarters, although it was about 200 miles away. He combed the accounting records looking for anything that would show the presence of a secretive operation, but everything appeared normal.

He decided next to work with each of the bookkeeping supervisors separately, using one to look into the Missouri location and the other the Indiana location.

The first supervisor was very willing to pull records for him on the Missouri operation. She noted that this factory was formerly the Gleaner Corporation. After a quiet conversation with some some well-placed flattery by Wilhelm, she said she would begin gathering files for him right away. She even told him she would work into the evening with him if it was required. He smiled broadly as he returned to his office.

The second supervisor was as enthusiastic to help him as the first had been. In fact, she was very familiar with the Indiana plant. They had acquired it in 1931 when it was the Rumely Company.

Wilhelm's ears perked up when he heard the word Rumely. *Plant R!* Wilhelm took an even greater interest in this supervisor, and she reacted by being ever more helpful.

Two days later, Wilhelm was combing the records for the La Porte Plant. Then he found it. At the end of last year, a large portion of the operations budget was set aside for new product development. The amount was larger than normal, but even more importantly, it was placed in a single well-hidden account with no detailed breakdown and no obvious oversight of spending. This had to be it.

He placed a call to the La Porte Plant asking for the individual in charge of new product development. His call was transferred to a superintendent by the name of Ray Herrington.

"Mr. Herrington, this is Walter Taylor at the Allis-Chalmers Headquarters. How are you today?"

"Very busy. How can I help you, Mr. Taylor?"

"Thank you for taking my call. I understand how busy production is for you these days. Ray, I'm an auditor performing a standard review of the books. You know how that goes." He laughed politely.

"Yes, you auditors aren't everyone's favorite people." He, too, laughed.

"The books show that expenses for your new product division are down significantly since the first of the year. Now, you know, I have to follow-up on anything out of the ordinary. So, a quick update from you should suffice." He paused waiting patiently for a response.

After an uncomfortable silence, Herrington spoke, "Well, with the way things are right now, our new product development efforts have been curtailed to some degree. You know, with this talk of war, the company is being cautious in new developments at this time." Now he paused, hoping he had said enough.

"I see. But it appears a budget transfer was made into your department at the end of last year." He paused without asking a question, again waiting for Herrington's reply. He felt this would tell him everything he needed.

"Plans change Mr. Taylor. I don't know what records you're looking at, but I no longer have that budget for the development of new tractors and farm equipment. As I said, those efforts have been put on hold. I'm sure that tells you all you need. If you'll excuse me, I'm late for a meeting. Have a good day, Mr. Taylor."

"You as well, Ray. Thank you." Wilhelm heard the call end before he even finished his sentence.

Wilhelm felt he had identified the location of Plant R where Allis-Chalmers was developing the new war machine. This was huge. He had to contact Duequesne and develop a plan. He knew he could not transfer his accounting role to the Indiana location. He would have to move in some other manner.

Before he contacted Duequesne, Wilhelm dug into the records specific to the new product development division at the La Porte Plant. With a little help from the supervisor and a little late night work, he was able to get a list of employees.

Wilhelm clearly understood his duty, and he was prepared to move forward. One week later, his accounting project in Milwaukee came to a quick conclusion. He packed his bags and left Wisconsin heading for La Porte, Indiana, where the new tank was under development. There, he would look into the lives of the men who were likely working on the tank. He needed to find the weak point to work his way into the secret project.

In Germany, Hitler had just invaded Poland. War had begun, and President Roosevelt committed to supporting Great Britain, although the U.S. would not yet directly enter the war effort.

Chapter 17

La Porte, 1939.

With the war in Europe expanding, activities picked up at Allis-Chalmers. Not only was there an increasing demand for farm equipment, but production of other machinery manufactured by the company was also increasing as Great Britain, among other Allied countries, felt a strong need to be fully prepared. The company found itself increasing production of more tractor and crawler equipment suitable for large construction projects.

Carl was pleased to be back working full-time with a busy workload of his own. His team was prototyping completely new continuous treads for the new tank that would handle the most difficult terrain. Power and strength to withstand punishing operations were paramount to all new development.

So, while the country was still in the Great Depression, work at Allis-Chalmers had picked up. It appeared that this talk of war was good for the company. It was good for Carl, and it was good for the town of La Porte.

Most everyone at the plant noticed frequent visits to the company by individuals they had never seen, obviously government officials. While not everyone was privy to all that was going on, most realized the United States Government was very interested in their work. Carl, of course, along with his team, knew the leading reason for their presence.

Recognition of Carl's skills was maintained within the small development team as he was still affectionately referred to as The Blacksmith. The name was well-received by Carl, and each member of the team would eventually have their own nickname. This helped develop a camaraderie among them, something greatly encouraged by the company at this time of ever-growing rumors of U.S. involvement in the war in Europe.

Carl was in his element offering keen insight into the new tank design. Carl was also using his skills in improving the production line itself. The engineers continued to be grateful to Carl for his sandwiched steel design and sought him out to improve upon other key design elements. This deep involvement was good for Carl as it kept him focused.

Respected by his co-workers, Carl made an effort to stop drinking. The effort was short-lived, however, as Carl felt he needed the drink to settle himself at times. Still, he was not drinking as much as he had been just a year ago.

Several nights each week, Carl stopped at the tavern before going home. On those nights, it was often late in the evening before Carl arrived at home. His daughter and mother-in-law were acutely aware of his drinking problem, but no longer talked about it. They did the best they could to take care of him. For his mother-in-law, this was more out of necessity than it was out of care. For his daughter, of course, it was truly out of love for her father.

This particular evening, Carl was sitting alone in a booth near the back of the tavern. He had already downed several drinks and had just ordered another when he was approached by a man who immediately reminded Carl of the many men in suits who had been coming and going at the plant.

"Say, aren't you Carl, the one they call The Blacksmith?" The man had a warm smile on his face and offered his hand to Carl.

"I could be. Who's asking?" Carl was a little cautious since he did not know how this man might be involved with the company . . . or perhaps the government. He did take the man's hand with a firm handshake, however. He noted that the man had large hands that were not calloused, but he did notice that the back of his hands and fingers were scarred. From this observation, Carl wondered to himself if the man was a former boxer. He certainly had the size and looks to be so.

"I'm sorry, Carl, the name is Gaines, William Gaines, but you can call me Bill." The man maintained the warm smile as he looked Carl in the eyes.

"Well, good evening, Bill. Yes, I'm Carl. And, yes, they do call me The Blacksmith at the plant." Carl dropped his air of caution giving in to the man's warmth and polite smile.

"It's a pleasure to meet you, Carl. May I sit?" Bill motioned to the bench on the opposite side of the booth.

Carl thought to himself that the man was mannerly for the ex-boxer Carl had made him out to be in his mind.

"Sure. What're you drinking? Let me buy you one." Carl's ego was boosted by the fact that the man seemed to know of Carl's reputation at work.

"I'll have whatever you're drinking, Carl. But, I insist on buying you the next drink."

Carl waved two fingers at the bartender who brought two whiskeys to the booth. He stood over the men waiting for payment. Carl pulled some money out of his pocket. The bartender counted out what he needed and returned to the bar. Carl was a bit embarrassed to have to pay when served rather than running a tab. The tavern had long ago learned to get Carl's payment up front or risk not getting paid.

Bill spoke up, "Thank you, Carl." Then he threw back his head and swallowed the drink. Carl did the same.

The man sat quietly looking at Carl waiting for Carl to speak next. Carl broke the brief silence, "So, how do you know my name?"

"It's just part of my job, Carl, to know important people." Again, the warm, admiring smile.

Bill looked to the bartender and waved his hand. The bartender approached the booth, and Bill ordered a bottle to be left for the two men.

"You don't need to do that, Mr. Gaines, uh, Bill. I can afford the drinks." Carl again felt embarrassed.

"Oh, Carl, I'm not trying to offend you. I've heard much about you, and I just want to be friendly and acknowledge your work at Allis-Chalmers." The man poured Carl a drink.

Carl looked at the glass and quickly drained it. Bill filled it again right away.

"Well, thanks. But, I'll ask again about how you know me." Carl downed the drink.

Again, the man filled Carl's glass as well as his own. He lifted his glass to Carl, and they both emptied their glasses.

"As I said, Carl, it's my business to know." He smiled as he poured another whiskey for Carl.

The drink was soothing Carl, and he found himself beginning to relax.

"Are you one of the men we've seen around the plant? Are you with the government monitoring the project?" Carl was now very pointed with his inquiry.

"You may have seen me at the plant, or you may not have. I really can't say anymore than that. With what you do know, Carl, I'm sure you understand." Bill flashed a reassuring smile as Carl finished another drink.

"Sure. What can you tell me, Bill? Why d'ya want to meet me?"

Bill filled Carl's glass. "Carl, we're aware of the work you do. You're very valuable to the production efforts at Allis-Chalmers. I just want you to know that your work is recognized at the highest levels. I guess I just wanted to meet The Blacksmith and say 'thank you.'" Bill was fully focused on Carl and spoke with great sincerity.

Carl was taken aback as he swallowed the overfilled glass. "I'm just part of the team. We're doing the best we can for the company." Speaking slowly, Carl sat back in the booth, now very relaxed. *No, Bill's not an ex-boxer.*

Carl did not remember much of the conversation after that. He remembered the man saying more kind things about Carl's work. He was fairly sure he thanked the man profusely.

When Carl had nearly passed out, Bill paid the bartender, including a large tip, then helped Carl to his car. He drove Carl home and helped him into his house. Carl unsteadily crossed the room to his chair where he flopped down and fell fast asleep.

Despite his heavy drinking, Carl arrived at work on time in the morning, Leona having awakened him when she awoke for work. Leona was twenty-one years old, but she still lived at home taking care of her father.

Carl wondered if any of his co-workers had been approached by one of the government men, but it seemed like something not to be discussed. So, the days continued as normal for the work group.

It was a week later when Bill again entered the tavern. Before approaching Carl, Bill stopped at the bar and ordered a bottle of whiskey. He then proceeded to the table where Carl was sitting alone.

"Hello, Carl. How are you?" As before, he offered his hand to Carl.

Carl immediately noticed Bill's engaging smile – and the bottle – and offered him a seat. Bill obliged, seating himself across from Carl. He placed the bottle down between them and opened it.

Carl began, "Bill, I wanted to thank you for taking me home last week. I guess I overdid it a bit." Carl ashamedly lowered his eyes as he spoke.

"Oh, Carl, it was nothing. I know how hard you work. We all have to let go once in a while." He poured a drink for both of them.

"Be that as it may, I won't put you in that position again." Carl was truly apologetic.

"Carl, that's water under the bridge." The man smiled broadly at Carl. He raised his glass to Carl, and they both drank.

As in their previous meeting, Bill freely poured drinks, always more drinks for Carl than for himself. Carl admired his generosity.

"So, Carl, I know you're of German ancestry. Has there been much anti-German sentiment with the growing war in Europe?" The smile had turned to a serious look.

Carl felt Bill's genuine interest in his welfare. "Not so much, Bill. Not at all like during the Great War. I was fortunate to live in La Porte. Germans were really well-accepted here."

"So, it's pretty quiet around here?"

"Yeah."

Bill frowned slightly bringing a thoughtful look to his face. "That's good to hear, Carl. It's not so good in many other areas. It's the same rhetoric leading to physical attacks in many of the larger cities." Bill was very serious now. "Fortunately, there are organizations watching out for the German-Americans in most of these places. It's just so sad to see it happening again, wouldn't you agree?" Bill intensely waited for an answer from Carl.

"Well, I guess, if it's as you say in other cities." Carl was unsure of himself answering the question.

"I'm glad you agree, Carl. We need good men of German heritage like yourself. You're doing a great deal for your country whether you realize it or not." Bill poured both of them a drink.

Bill changed the subject. "Do you remember coming to America, Carl?"

"I guess I haven't thought about it in a long time. I was only about ten years old." Carl had that far away look as he searched his memory. "I sure don't remember anything much pleasant about it."

"It was a tough journey, for sure," Bill sympathized.

"Wait. You came over from Germany?" Carl was quite surprised. "Bill Gaines. That's certainly not a German name."

"Oh, like so many German immigrants, it was changed along the way."

Feeling a closeness with Bill, Carl inquired, "What was your German name?"

"Oh, that's not important any longer. It fell out of use more years ago than I can remember." Bill had a faint distant look in his eyes as though recalling a past memory.

"When did you come over?" Carl was now curious.

"Oh, let's see, it was about 1879 – no, it was 1880. I was only about five years old. I really don't remember much."

"I came over in 1890, ten years later," Carl shared his own memory.

"1890, huh? Well, my family had returned to Germany briefly, and I came back to the States from that trip in . . . yes, it was in 1890."

"Well, so you came here for the second time as I was coming for the first time." Carl's eyes lit up a bit.

"Sounds about right." Bill smiled at Carl.

They both took another drink, and Bill refilled Carl's glass.

After a moment of thoughtfulness, Bill continued speaking, "I did get involved in an incident on the ship on that second voyage. There was a bad group of young men running about freely in steerage taking advantage of some of the weaker families." He paused as he searched his memory. "I suppose this happened on a lot of ships." He paused again and noticed the attention from Carl. "Well, I saw them assaulting a man with a young child at his side. It was a terrible thing. The young ruffian tore through the man's belongings scattering them across the deck. He then found a large amount of cash on the man and took it. He actually hit the small boy in the melee. It was more than I could bear. I jumped in taking down the young brute and one of his friends. As I recall, I beat them soundly and recovered what I could of the man's money. I felt so sorry for that family." He paused and looked aside as if he had just relived the event.

Carl was dumbfounded. "My God, Bill. What ship were you on?"

Bill searched his memory. "Let's see. It was a German vessel." Bill searched his memory again. "Uh, let's see. It was . . . It began with a G . . ."

"*Gellert*!" Carl spit out. "Was it the *Gellert*?!" Carl was excited.

Bill paused to confirm his memory before replying, "Yes, Carl, it was the *Gellert*. How did you know that?"

"That man was my father! That boy was me!" Carl stood up with excitement. "It was me, Bill. You saved my father and me!"

Bill smiled broadly. "Carl, I know a lot about you, but I didn't know this. I'm astonished. What are the odds?!" The two celebrated with drinks well into the night.

Chapter 18

La Porte, 1939-1940.

Innovation continued throughout the early days of the second World War as it came to be known. Production at Allis-Chalmers became focused on the war effort, with the La Porte plant taking on a critical role in the production of standard tractor and tracked hauling equipment for construction efforts.

Of course, the new armored tank destroyer for the government was the critical, and secretive, project for Carl and the Rubber Tire team. It was the most secretive project the La Porte Plant had ever undertaken. Even though security was tightly controlled, it had become obvious to the workers that the heavily guarded building must be doing something for the war. However, no one on the Rubber Tire team had divulged any information.

Carl and his fellow workers were provided with additional classified identification cards issued directly from the federal government. All personal items were searched upon entry and exit to their secure area of the plant. U.S. military personnel were permanently stationed at the plant twenty-four hours of every day.

Carl continued his friendship with Bill, and they still met at least one night per week at the tavern. While Carl completely trusted Bill, he knew that he could not discuss his current project with him. However, Carl suspected that Bill likely knew most everything about the project. He was probably assigned to keep an eye on several individuals on the team. Carl also thought that perhaps he was under additional scrutiny because of his drinking habit. Maybe there was a concern that he would say more than he should. If that was the case, it was fine with Carl. Bill seemed to be a nice guy.

"Carl, you must be working on something really special if you can't even talk to me about it." The two were in a very relaxed mood at the bar.

"Bill, you know I simply can't talk about my work any longer. Now that the war has started in Europe, we're under even tighter control at the plant." Carl stated the obvious and wondered if perhaps he was being tested.

In September of 1939, Germany had invaded Poland marking the start of the war. France and Great Britain declared war on Germany two days later. The United States sided with the Allies but was staying out of the war at this time. While most of the public opposed any military intervention by the U.S., behind the scenes, America was preparing to fully support the Allies with aid and assets. Expecting the war to grow, the government was also preparing advanced military equipment at numerous facilities around the country.

"I know, Carl. You also know I'm not just some guy off the streets. I know more about the efforts of American manufacturing than you're aware of." Bill paused and poured Carl a drink. "Like you, I can't say much either." Bill poured Carl another drink after he had finished the previous one. "I guess we both know what we know and won't share it. We'll have to leave it at that." Bill laughed, and Carl did the same.

Carl really appreciated having a friend outside of his work group with whom he could talk. He was feeling the stress of the long hours and short deadlines at work. The additional security on top of everything else only added to the anxiety he felt. As a result, Carl fell even deeper into drink.

"Bill, I wish I could say more, but it's nice to have a friend to talk with. I do appreciate that very much." Carl lifted his glass to Bill and took another drink.

As with many of their late nights together, Bill had to help Carl home. This night Carl got out of the car in front of his house and made his way in by himself. He waved at Bill as the car drove off.

This seemed to be their routine over the next weeks that became months. They did discuss the growing war in general. In November 1939, the U.S. increased its efforts in support of the Allies and, specifically, to China after it had been invaded by Japan.

As 1939 turned into 1940, Bill told Carl he needed to talk to him about a serious matter. Bill asked Carl to meet him at a restaurant on the east end of town. It was a little nicer place than the small neighborhood tavern to which Carl was accustomed.

Carl immediately noticed the seriousness of Bill's expression as he joined him at a table near the back of the bar area. "Sit down, Carl." The seriousness continued in Bill's tone.

Carl sat down and continued looking into Bill's eyes. "Bill, what's going on? What's wrong?"

Bill poured them both a drink. He downed his quickly, and Carl followed suit. He then poured them both another drink.

"Look, Carl, I haven't been completely straight with you." Bill paused as if searching for his words. "Carl, I haven't told you a lot about my work for good reason. But, now, I need to bring you in on what I'm doing." He again paused and took a drink. "Carl, I need you to swear that you will not reveal anything I'm about to tell you to anyone." He was looking very directly into Carl's eyes.

"Bill, certainly, you can count on me." Carl was puzzled.

"Carl, I mean it. This is very serious . . . it's of national interest. I have to have more than 'count on me.' I need your loyalty . . . loyalty to me and loyalty to your country." He paused with his eyes fixed on Carl. "Can you do this?" Bill leaned back in his chair as if exhausted.

"Bill, I don't understand. I've told you I'm working under strict secrecy of the government at work. Of course, you can trust my loyalty." Carl was very serious in his reply. "What do you need?"

Bill leaned forward and pulled his wallet from his suit coat. He opened it to Carl revealing a government identification. It indicated Bill was a special agent of the Federal Bureau of Investigation for the U.S. Government. Bill placed his wallet back in his coat. Leaning closer across the table, Bill spoke quietly, "Carl, you must not reveal what I just showed you to anyone. Do you understand?"

Carl was stunned. "Of course, Bill."

"Good." Bill paused, and Carl was unsure what to do or say next. It seemed like they simply stared at one another forever.

Carl finally broke the silence. "What do you want to tell me, Bill?"

"Here it is, Carl. I know all about the work you do. I'm part of a high-security team that is protecting the very project on which you're working." He paused again, searching for his words. He poured Carl another drink. "Carl, this isn't easy to say. I've been testing you. I've done everything I could to get you to talk about your project. I needed to know that you were truly someone we could trust."

"Bill, I don't know what to say. Our friendship has all been just a test. You were using me?!" Carl's voice grew louder.

"No, Carl . . . I mean, initially, I had to test you . . . but we did grow into good friends. I really mean that Carl. You've got to believe me." Bill looked around to see if anyone had noticed their conversation.

Carl was shaking his head. "Bill, I really felt I could talk to you as a friend. I've probably been closer to you than anyone. Outside of work, there's really no one else. But now, it feels like it was all just an act." It was obvious that Carl was trying to remain calm as he spoke, but again the level of his voice was rising.

Bill kept his tone low, "Carl, I'm sorry. But, please, believe me, you are my friend. I appreciate what we have together. Look, haven't I helped you home on numerous occasions? Carl, I've taken care of you because you are my friend."

Carl downed several drinks and slammed the glass on the table. "Geez, Bill, I don't know what to think." He sat there staring at the glass in front of him.

"Look, Carl, I've told you this because I know I can trust you. I know I can trust you because you're my friend. You have to understand, with the war going on, we have to be cautious. You must understand that knowing the very project you're working on." Bill appealed longingly to Carl.

Carl calmed down. "Bill, why are you telling me this now?"

Bill straightened himself before again leaning in to Carl. "Carl, there's someone in your company who is trying to get access to the work you're doing. We believe a German spy is trying to get the plans for your project." He wanted to let that sink in a bit before providing more details to Carl.

Carl was dumbfounded. He could barely comprehend what he had just been told. *A German spy at work?!*

Bill understood the look on Carl's face. "We're quite sure, Carl. I've been working on this even before the day we met." Then he dropped the rest of his news on Carl. "We need someone on the inside who we know we can trust. We feel you are that person, Carl."

Carl was stunned. "Me? Me?! What can I do? Sure, I've got a great understanding of what we're doing, but how could I possibly help you with this spy? I don't know, Bill." Carl was shaking his head back and forth.

"Carl, trust me, we wouldn't be asking this of you if we didn't feel we could trust you. Carl, you've proven to me that you can be trusted. We need you for this, Carl."

Carl continued shaking his head. He took another drink. "Bill, this is all too much. I just don't know."

"That's exactly why you're the right person. You're always simply yourself. We can't risk trying to put one of our own people into the group. It would arouse too many suspicions. Carl, tell me you'll work with me."

"But what would I have to do?"

"Carl, it would be simple. We'll have a false set of plans in place. You'll pick them up for us, then we can identify and confront the spy. It's all quite simple, but let's not talk about that for now." He stopped and tried to calm Carl. "Tell you what, I've thrown a lot at you tonight. Why don't you mull it over. We can meet back here Monday evening for super, and we can talk some more. Would that be okay, Carl?"

"Uh, yeah, I guess." Carl was looking down.

"Let's leave it at that, then, Carl. In the meantime, I'm sorry, but you just can't share any of this with anyone. Are we good, Carl?" His tone was comforting.

"Yeah, sure." Carl finished his drink, pushed back his chair, and stood. "See ya Monday."

Carl thought a lot about Bill's proposal over the weekend. There was no one he could talk with about this. Here he was of German heritage and being asked by the United States Government to help capture a German spy. He pondered this with a bottle, drinking more than usual.

At the same time, Carl felt his father's presence pushing him to stay out of this thing that would only further tarnish Germans. His father had remained loyal to Germany even after expressing his desire to make a new life in America when they had first arrived. His following of German newspapers and association with pro-German organizations had caused him problems as the Great War approached. It had all left a bitter taste in his father's mouth that had never gone away. Carl even felt that it had contributed to his father's death.

Carl drank himself to sleep Sunday night with thoughts of being a hero who helped out his adopted country.

Monday evening, Carl met with Bill at the restaurant on the east side of town. Carl thought he was ready to do whatever Bill was going to ask of him, but as he neared the restaurant, he felt the doubt creep in.

He entered and searched for Bill, spotting him in the back at the same table that they had met at previously. Bill had a bottle already waiting on the table, and Carl was glad to see it. Bill poured drinks as Carl approached. Immediately upon sitting, Carl palmed the glass and finished it quickly. Bill poured him another.

"Bill, I thought I was ready to do this, but now I'm not sure."

"Relax, Carl. Have another drink. I assume you gave this a lot of thought over the weekend?" Bill's tone was reassuring.

"Yeah, I did. But, I'm a little scared about this, Bill. What if I get caught. They'll think I'm actually stealing the plans." Carl appeared very nervous.

Bill poured another drink for Carl. "Look, as I said, we'll have a false set of plans in place. All you have to do is take those and pass them along. It will be simple and easy. As soon as you pass them to the contact, our guys come in and make the arrest. You'll be a real hero, Carl!" He reached across the table and slapped Carl on the shoulder.

"Okay, tell me more about how this will work." Carl was still hesitant.

"You just go on about your work normally. I can't tell you exactly when, but as soon as you get a new set of drawings for your project, you'll know the plan has been activated. After work, you place one of the copies of the plans in a new lunch pail we'll provide for you. It will have a false bottom. You'll have to tightly fold the plans and place them in the pail. You leave work as normal." Bill paused to be sure Carl understood. "Good so far?"

"Sure, but then what do I do?"

"You'll go through your normal routine. Stop at your regular watering hole where a man will approach you. He'll sit and have a drink with you. Then he'll leave with your lunch pail.

When he leaves the bar, we nab him, and its all over." He smiled at Carl and waited for a response.

"Okay, I guess it sounds easy enough." As he took another drink, he once again thought about being a hero.

Chapter 19

For the next several days at work, Carl was obviously nervous about the situation. He continued to have doubts about what Bill had asked him to do. When his co-workers noticed Carl's demeanor, they simply felt it was Carl's drinking. Most thought that perhaps he was trying to stop drinking now that they were working on the secret government project. So, with that thought, they ignored his uneasiness.

Each day, Carl wanted to see a new set of plans so that this whole thing would be finished. He wondered what was taking so long, or if there had been a change in the arrangements. He had hoped to see Bill at the tavern, but he had not come by.

Then, the following week, a new set of drawings with some changes were delivered to the group. Carl felt his level of fear growing. At each reference to the new plans, Carl felt sick. He was almost afraid to even touch the drawings.

The team gathered around a table and spread out one of the copies of the plans. They discussed the changes, most of which seemed to be very minor. Carl did not have anything to say. Again, the others ignored the change in his character and went about their own work.

At the end of the day, all copies of the plans were placed in a file, and the cabinet was locked. Carl, knew, however, that the simple filing cabinet could easily be opened. That would not present a problem to him.

As they were all leaving for the day, Carl told the others that he had forgotten his lunch pail, and he would have to go back to get it. He returned to their work area and closed the door behind him. He went into the next room where the files were kept. He was breathing heavily and sweating. He longed for a drink.

He paused in the doorway as doubts entered his mind. He tried to overcome his doubts telling himself this would be over very shortly. He took several deep breaths and approached the filing cabinet where the new set of plans was located. He was thinking about how to get them folded tightly enough to fit into the false bottom of his lunch pail which he had retrieved as he entered the office. He looked at the lunch pail in his hand. He then again looked at the filing cabinet. *I can do this.*

He reached into his pocket for a pen knife that he always carried. He could easily pop the simple lock with the knife. He stopped in front of the filing cabinet containing his objective. As he unfolded the knife, he heard someone enter through the main door to the work area. Carl froze in fear. *Who could that be? Why are they here?*

He heard footsteps approaching the room he was in. *Stupid! I never should have turned the lights on!* Sweat beaded on his forehead as he stood silently.

"Carl, you in here?" Carl recognized the voice of one of his co-workers.

Carl could not respond. He opened his mouth, but no words would come out. The footsteps began again, and Carl knew the man was nearing the doorway. Carl forced himself to breathe.

"Yeah, in here. I guess I left my lunch pail in here." Carl turned and walked out of the room after putting his knife back into his pocket. He held up the lunch pail as he left the file room.

"Carl, you look like shit. Are you feeling okay? We've all noticed you haven't been yourself lately." The man was sincerely concerned.

"Yeah, I'm fine. Just a bit under the weather, I guess." Carl wiped his brow with his sleeve.

"Well, get to feelin' better." The man raised the dented lunch pail he was holding in his own hand. "You weren't the only one who forgot his pail. I see you got a new one there." He approached Carl and patted him on the back before Carl could respond. "Carl, go home tonight and get some rest." With his arm, he led Carl toward the door.

Outside the plant, the men said their good-byes. Carl could not wait for them to leave. He walked around the next corner and threw up. He badly wanted a drink, but he could not go to the bar. He went home where he drank deeply; and seriously frightened, he sobbed as he fell into a deep sleep.

Carl went to work the next day expecting to answer questions about the previous night, but no one said a thing. In Carl's mind, the events of last night loomed large, but it was really nothing to the others. No one even asked Carl how he was feeling.

Carl could not bring himself to make another attempt to obtain the plans. He did not know what he was going to tell Bill. Two nights later, Bill approached Carl in the bar.

"Carl, how are you?" As usual, his tone was upbeat.

Bill sat down. Carl was nearly bursting as he spoke in a loud whisper, "Bill, I almost got caught! I almost got caught!"

Bill looked around the room and leaned in toward Carl, "Carl, be quiet. You have to be quiet. Now, tell me what happened. I need to hear every detail."

Bill listened intently as Carl provided every bit of detail about his failure to procure the phony plans. Carl was excited, scared, and also remorseful that he had not come through for Bill.

"I'm so sorry, Bill. But, I haven't been the same since this happened. At work, they think I'm sick. I'm not myself. Bill, I'm done with this! I'm so sorry." He stopped, having felt like he had poured his guts out to Bill.

"I'm really sorry to hear this, Carl. Let's table this plan for now. You need to settle back down into a normal routine. Carl, don't think any more about this. You did fine. This could have happened to even the best of men. You handled it like a pro. We'll just have to come up with a new plan. Carl, just let this go and get back to your normal routine. You should be proud at even having attempted this for your country. It was just a simple circumstance that got in the way." He looked Carl confidently in the eyes assuring him that all was fine.

"Thanks, Bill. I'm just so sorry." Carl ashamedly lowered his head.

"I know you are, Carl. Look, just sit tight and enjoy your drink, I need to go. I hope we'll talk again soon." Bill reached out for Carl's hand as he stood. He grabbed it firmly and shook it several times while smiling at Carl.

Carl's head leaned forward to the glass in front of him. He felt like a failure. He could hear his father's voice telling him he would amount to nothing if he left the farm.

"You are nothing but a farmer. Don't try to make yourself anything more than that! Sie sind ein idiot!"

"Nein, Papa. I can make my own way! The other farmers respect me as a blacksmith. They ask for my help. I am leaving!"

Carl slammed his fist down on the table. He raised his head and looked around. No one seemed to take notice of him. He poured himself one drink and then another and another.

Carl did not notice the four men who had taken seats at the table just behind him to his right. As he neared the end of the bottle, Carl was talking loudly to himself.

"Hero! Yes! Tell me about German spies. I am a good German! Ha! I am a good American. I will get those plans! They'll see . . . they'll see."

One of the four men approached Carl. "Hey, Carl. You've had a bit much, buddy."

"What much? You talkin' to me? Hmmph."

"Carl, I work at the plant. Jacob, who works with you, thought you might need looking after."

"Jacob! Good man, Jacob. No, no, you're not Jacob."

"No, Carl, I'm James. Jacob's sitting right over there." He pointed to the table where the three other men were sitting.

"Well, why didn't you say so?! Jacob, come join us!" Carl waved his arm in the air.

The other three men came over to Carl's table, and Jacob now took the lead.

"Carl, why don't you finish that drink and let us give you a ride home? Okay?"

Carl stared up at Jacob who was standing next to James. "Jacob, I think I should have another drink. Why don't you all join me. How many of you are there swaying in front of me?" Carl laughed and finished his drink. He then lifted the bottle and swallowed the remaining light brown liquid.

Jacob and James each grabbed one of Carl's arms and lifted him to his feet.

"Come on, Carl. We'll help you home."

In the parking lot, the four men and Carl got into a large dark sedan. Carl was in the back seat between Jacob and James. Carl's head slumped, but James lifted his head and made sure Carl was alert.

"Carl, buddy, stay awake. We want to ask you some questions."

Carl turned toward James. "Everyone wants to ask me questions. What do I know? I don't know anything! Just ask Papa! Ha!" Carl stared at James. "Do I know you? Where's Jacob?"

"I'm here, Carl."

Carl shifted all his weight as he turned to Jacob on his left. "There you are. Hey, we got our lunch pails!"

"Yes, Carl. You have a new one, remember?"

"Yes. A brand new lunch pail. My friend Bill got it for me. But, I can't tell anyone. Bill is a big shot, you know. But I can't say a word. Bill helped me, and now he wants me to help him."

James pulled on Carl's shoulder and asked, "And just who is your friend Bill? It seems you've met him at the bar a number of times." He lifted Carl's chin with his hand. "Who is he Carl? What kind of help does he want?"

"Well, Bill is my friend! I'm helping Bill. I can't say any-more. My lips are sealed." Carl leaned back in the seat, but James immediately pulled him forward. "Carl, we need more than that."

The car came to a stop at the end of a long gravel driveway. All the men got out of the car, and James pulled Carl along by one arm.

They went to the rear of the house and opened a cellar door. The first man turned on a light as the other men entered the low, cool room. Jacob was now forcing Carl along as he stumbled. He forced Carl to sit in a chair. One of the other men wrapped a rope around Carl and secured him to the chair.

"What's going on here! Let me alone!"

James threw a punch that caught Carl on the chin sending his head to one side. The other men made sure the chair did not tip over.

"You son-of-a . . ." was all Carl could manage before he was struck again.

"Now, Carl," James spat, "tell us more about your friend, Bill. Why are you meeting with him?"

"He's just one of the government men at the plant. That's all. I swear!" Carl was suddenly very alert despite the effects of the alcohol.

Jacob spoke up, "Carl, what were you doing when you went back for your lunch pail? Why were you in the file room where all the plans are kept? What were you really up to, Carl?!"

James immediately struck Carl across the face with the back of his hand. "Talk, you Nazi bastard!"

Carl now had tears streaming down his cheeks. "Nazi?! What are you talking about?! I'm not a Nazi! Are you guys nuts?!" Carl cried out loudly.

Jacob spoke quietly to Carl. "Then just tell us what you were doing and who your friend is, Carl. You can clear all of this up for us so easily."

"I told you, he's just one of the government big shots. He likes how well we're doing."

"Carl, there are rumors that the Nazis have spies in the plant. Carl, is Bill a Nazi spy?" Jacob paused. "Are you a Nazi spy?!"

James once again back-handed Carl.

Carl continued sobbing and spat blood from his mouth. "We have to stop the Nazis." Carl spoke very quietly between sobs. "I will be a hero. You'll see."

This time Jamess threw a hard punch to Carl's head knocking Carl unconscious.

"He's a stupid, drunken nothing. Untie him and let's take him home."

Fifteen minutes later, the dark sedan crawled slowly in front of Carl's house. A rear door opened, and Carl spilled out into his front yard.

Chapter 20

The next day, Carl was at work right on time. The previous night's activities took their toll on Carl, but he still managed to get to work just as he did when he had been drinking heavily. The security guard stopped Carl before he could enter the secured area.

"Carl, what the hell happened to you?" He closely examined the bruises on Carl's face as Carl tried to back away.

"Oh, just a little fall at home. I'll be fine."

"Well, before you go in today, the superintendent needs to see you in his office. I was told to bring you there."

"Sure, fine." Carl, tired and feeling defeated, willingly submitted to the guard.

The two men made their way to an office on the second floor. A sign on the door simply read, "Mr. Herrington." The guard knocked on the door.

"Yes, come in."

The guard opened the door and showed Carl in.

"Mr. Herrington, Carl Schmidt is here."

"Thank you, Bob. That'll be all." His head had been down looking at some papers on his desk. He lifted his eyes to Carl and was surprised by his bruised face. "Oh my, Carl, what happened to you?"

Carl looked about the room. The executive sat behind his large wooden desk covered with several neat piles of paper, and there in one of the two leather chairs in front of the desk was Jacob. Carl looked over at Jacob who quickly averted his eyes.

"Just a bad fall at home, sir. I'll be fine."

"Well, I hope you at least got a lick in on the other guy!" and Mr. Herrington laughed. "Carl, please sit down." His tone had quickly turned serious.

Carl made his way to the open chair next to Jacob. He noticed that Jacob would not look at him.

Mr. Herrington returned his eyes to the papers on his desk. "Carl, Jacob has brought me some troubling information. I'm sure it's all a simple misunderstanding that we can clear up. Okay?" He looked up at Carl.

"Yes, sir."

"Now, Jacob here tells me you were seen in a secure area after hours. He also said you've been meeting with a man by the name of Bill outside of work. A man who is, uh, how can I put this, someone above your means." He tapped his fingers on the solid wooden desk. "Jacob seems to feel there's something nefarious going on between you and this man that has to do with your access in the secure area." He looked at Jacob and said, "Does that about sum it up, Jacob?"

Jacob kept his eyes down as he answered, "Yes, uh, yes, sir."

"Now, Carl, I'm sure you can easily clear this up for us." He left the open-ended statement hanging in the air waiting for Carl to reply.

Carl felt sweat building on his brow. He wiped his forehead with his sleeve. "Well, sir, I think Jacob is just confused about this whole thing." Carl stopped and cleared his dry throat. *What I wouldn't give for a drink right now.* "I just can't really talk about it here." He again wiped his brow.

"Well, Carl, I don't know how we clear this up if you won't tell us what's going on. Do you understand?"

Carl shifted in his chair and nervously rubbed his hands together.

"Carl, you seem to be unnerved by this. I'm sorry, but I can't help but think that there's something more that you aren't telling me. Now, can we clear this up, or will I have to take this to a higher level?" His tone was serious, even threatening to Carl.

"Well, you see, uh, . . ." Carl fought for his words, "Can I talk to you alone without Jacob here?" He looked over at Jacob who was still staring at the floor.

Mr. Herrington looked serious. "Jacob, why don't you go on to work now. I'll clarify the situation with Carl."

Jacob slowly stood, and Mr. Herrington rose to show him to the door.

"I'm sorry, Carl," Jacob spoke softly as he walked behind Carl.

Mr. Herrington returned to his chair behind the large desk.

"Okay, Carl, it's just you and me. Now, let's clear this up, shall we?"

"Mr. Herrington, I have an idea of what Jacob has told you, but I assure you it is nothing like that at all. You've got to believe me!" Carl pleaded.

"Carl, I'm growing impatient. Quit stumbling around and talk to me!"

Carl straightened in his chair as Mr. Herrington took on a much more aggressive tone.

"Well, you see, uh, the thing is, I, uh, it's a bit complicated."

"Then unravel it for me Carl, and do it soon!"

Carl wiped his brow again. *I wonder if Mr. Herrington keeps a bottle in that desk.* "Well, the man Jacob told you I was meeting with, Bill, well, William Gaines, is an agent with the FBI." Carl stopped there hoping that was enough to satisfy Mr. Herrington.

Mr. Herrington looked intensely at Carl. "Go on."

"Well, that's about all I can say. You see, everything else Bill told me is part of a special investigation he's working on." Suddenly, Carl felt himself speaking rapidly. "He's familiar with our work, and with me personally, and he's trying to keep us all safe. He's a good man, and I'm a good person. I'm not a Nazi!" Carl put his face in his hands and sobbed.

"Carl, that's an interesting start, but we need to get to the bottom of this. I'm calling Mr. Scholl. If this Mr. Gaines is who he says he is, Mr. Scholl will know."

Half an hour later, a half hour that seemed like an entire day to Carl, he and Mr. Herrington were seated at a conference table in a very well-appointed room that served the president and his executive officers. Mr. Scholl appeared at a side entrance, apparently from his office next door. Mr. Herrington rose to meet Mr. Scholl, so Carl followed suit.

"Good morning, Ray. How are you?" Mr. Scholl extended his hand and a very warm smile to Mr. Herrington.

"Just fine, sir. Thank you for working in a meeting with us on such short notice." He paused and introduced Carl. "Mr. Scholl, this is Carl Schmidt. As I told you, he's one of the men working in our high security area on Project Rubber Tire."

Mr. Scholl greeted Carl in the same manner as he had Mr. Herrington. Carl responded cordially.

"Carl, I am very much aware of your contributions to the team. As I understand it, you are the one they call The Blacksmith, are you not?"

"Yes, sir, that's correct," Carl replied meekly.

Mr. Scholl smiled pleasantly at both men. "Let's sit, gentlemen, and you can brief me on what this urgent meeting is all about."

Mr. Herrington provided the limited detail he had concerning the situation as Carl looked on, occasionally wiping his brow. He noticed that Mr. Scholl listened with great intensity. It was obvious that he would not miss a word.

"Carl, I hope you understand how serious this situation is. Mr. Herrington went so far as to suggest I have a security man outside the door of this meeting. Do you understand why we are so concerned? Do you really understand?" His smile was gone, and his brow was wrinkled.

"Yes, sir, I do understand, and I want this all cleared up." Carl nervously fidgeted with the buttons on his shirt.

"Now, you say this Agent William Gaines is involved in a special investigation, and he has pulled you in to aid him?"

"Yes, sir. He told me not to say anything about this to anyone. He made me swear."

"Carl, I am made aware of every move the government agencies are making in our La Porte Plant. If there were an investigation involving our plant, I would be made fully aware of it. Doesn't that make sense to you that the company's highest officer would be read in on any such investigations?"

"Well, I, uh, guess so."

"Carl, let me bluntly ask you this, and I want complete honesty from you. Are you working with a German spy?" Mr. Scholl was looking intently into Carl's eyes. He seemed to be studying Carl as a doctor might be examining a patient.

Tears began to well up in Carl's eyes. "No, Mr. Scholl, I am not a spy. I am not working with a spy. I am a good American trying to help the United States of America."

Mr. Scholl leaned back in his chair and pondered Carl's remarks. "I believe you, Carl." He paused and leaned forward toward Carl. "Now give me every detail of what has gone on with this Agent Gaines." Mr. Scholl had a stenographer come in to transcribe Carl's statement.

For the next hour, Carl shared everything he could recall. He felt bad that some details were missing because of his drunkenness. When he told the two men about his attempt to remove the plans from the building, Carl broke down in tears. When he was finished, Carl felt as though a weight had been lifted from his shoulders.

"Carl, I had my office check with the FBI while you were talking. There is no Special Agent William Gaines anywhere within the FBI. Mr. Gaines is not an FBI agent. Carl, I told you that I believed you, but I have to ask you one more time. We know that part of this story is not true, so we have to continue to get to the bottom of this."

Mr. Herrington broke in, "He's obviously already lied about this Gaines character. You can't trust anything he says. He's a liar and a traitor to this country. He's likely exactly what his accusers have said . . . a Nazi!" Mr. Herrington pounded the table with his hand.

"Settle down, Ray. I'm inclined to believe that Carl was led astray by an experienced con man, and yes, likely a spy. The FBI is on their way here, and they will interview Carl." He turned to Carl who was now despondent. "Carl, we'll let the FBI – the real FBI – interview you, and we'll see what they have to say. I appreciate how you have opened up to us, and we will share the transcription with them before they meet with you. We have agreed to let you remain in this room. The security guard will remain outside."

Mr. Scholl stood, and Mr. Herrington followed suit. "Is there anything we can get for you while you're waiting, Carl?"

A good stiff drink would sure be good. "I could use some water, if that's not too much trouble."

Carl's head was down reflecting the way he felt. He thought that once he told the men everything, they would be done, and he could go back to work. Now, he would have to do it all over again with the FBI. *How could I have been so stupid! Who is Bill Gaines?!*

"Sure, Carl. It may be a few hours before the FBI arrives. We'll get some lunch for you before then as well. Okay?"

"Yes, sir, thank you."

The two men left the room, and Carl laid his head on the table and cried. He felt so alone.

Three hours later, after Carl had eaten a sandwich, the door from the hallway burst open. Three men in black suits strode confidently into the room. They ordered Carl to stand, and one of the men patted him down and searched his pockets.

They moved a single chair off to the side of the table and ordered Carl to sit in the chair. Carl was tired and nervous as he blindly followed their orders. One man set up a transcription machine much like the one used earlier by Mr. Scholl's office.

After Carl sat, one of the men told Carl to remove his shoes. He untied them and set them next to his chair. The man took his shoes and placed them well away from Carl after closely examining them. This was all very confusing to Carl.

After organizing piles of paper on the conference room table, one of the men finally spoke to Carl. "Mr. Schmidt, I am Agent Smith with the FBI. Over there is Agent Jones, and sitting at the transcription machine is Agent White. We're going to begin now."

With his head slightly down, the man lifted his eyes and looked at Carl as if asking for a recognition of what he had just said. Carl looked back at the man with an understanding that these men would remain anonymous as Smith, Jones, and White. Carl would never know their real names. That only added to Carl's confusion and allowed some fear to creep into his mind.

The interrogation was grueling, nothing at all like the meeting with Mr. Herrington and Mr. Scholl. The men asked him questions about his family, his wife, his children, his parents. They asked why his family had left Germany. Had he ever been back? Did he desire to go back? Did he correspond with friends? Carl did not understand how any of this related to the situation with Bill.

After an hour of this line of questioning, the men turned to questions about his job, and they wanted to know all about his job history back to his work on his father's farm. This led to detailed questions about his father and his feelings about Germany. They were very interested in the newspapers he had read.

After another hour, they began asking the same questions over and over. Carl felt like they were trying to confuse him and trip him up over his own words.

Another hour went by. Carl was soaked with sweat, and so were the FBI agents. They smoked heavily, but never offered

Carl a cigarette. Carl wondered why they were not asking about Bill Gaines. More questions about his work, then his family, then newspapers, then what he did in his off time, then the same thing over and over. Carl was exhausted and wanted to know when they would be finished. The men did not bother responding to him.

Another hour went by, and they finally got around to asking about Bill Gaines. Carl shared every bit of information he could recall. Again, the questions were repeated over and over. Carl's head was pounding. He needed a break. Again he asked, and again he was ignored.

The men finally asked Carl to describe Bill Gaines. They prodded for every detail possible. Their questioning slowed down as they wanted to create a complete description of the man.

Then, suddenly, "We're done here." The agent didn't even really say this to Carl.

The agent at the transcription machine began packing the equipment. Carl sat still as the men began gathering all of their notes.

"Carl," now the agent looked at Carl, "are you certain the man's identification did not contain a badge number?"

"I'm sorry," Carl said tiredly, "I just never thought to look for one. The identification looked very official with the FBI logo. I'm sorry." Carl's head fell to his chest.

"Carl, you are not to leave town. You are to continue to come to work. You cannot say anything about any of this to anyone other than us, Mr. Scholl, and Mr. Herrington. Nobody else, Carl. For now, you will not meet with Bill Gaines. Do you understand?"

"Yes."

Two of the men exited the room. As the third agent prepared to exit, he turned to Carl. "Carl, for what it's worth, you did very well. We believe your story. We also believe you have had contact with a key member of a Nazi spy ring working within the United States."

Carl lifted his head to see the man's eyes.

"He used you, Carl. He took advantage of your trusting nature and your desire to help your country. We will bring this man down, Carl. We're still thinking this through, but we may need to keep you involved with him."

Carl perked up, not because the idea interested him, but rather because it scared him. *How could I manage this after what has happened? Wouldn't Bill see right through me? No, don't ask me to do this!*

"Go home and get some rest, we'll be in touch with the company in a day or two with our plan for the next steps. Thank you, Carl."

Carl sat alone, exhausted and frightened. He craved a drink.

Chapter 21

Three days later, the FBI rolled out their proposal. The plan would be limited on a need-to-know basis to Carl, Mr. Scholl, and Mr. Herrington. No one else in the company would know of the arrangement. There would be a single point of contact with the FBI through Special Agent Al Jeffers from the Chicago office. Special Agent Jeffers would remain in La Porte to the conclusion. Other agents would be part of the plan, but this was not made known to Carl, Mr. Scholl, or Mr. Herrington.

Carl was the key to the success of the plan. He must continue his contact with Bill Gaines. He must be cautious not to arouse suspicion, but at the same time he would need to convince Gaines that he needed more time to get the blueprints to him.

Special Agent Jeffers assured Carl that he would be under close watch at all times. He need not fear for his safety, or that of his family, in any way.

Carl was nervous to say the least. He coped with the situation in his usual manner, by drinking heavily. This certainly did not arouse any suspicions among his workers as it was not unusual for Carl to drink heavily at the end of his work day.

The men Carl worked with were told that their suspicions about Carl were unfounded, but they did not seem to be satisfied. They continued to be suspicious of Carl and were, at best, uncooperative with him and would not associate with him. Carl felt more isolated than ever.

Two nights later at the tavern, Bill Gaines approached Carl who was already seated. As he usually did, Bill brought a full bottle of good whiskey to the table. Carl looked up as he motioned Bill to sit, although he was already in the process of sitting without Carl's offer.

Bill opened the bottle, refilled Carl's glass, and poured a drink for himself. He lifted his glass to Carl and threw the drink down his throat. Carl watched Bill before swallowing his own drink. Bill refilled the glasses.

"Carl, how are you doing? You look a little down."

"You don't know the half of it. Look closely, and you can still see the bruises on my face."

Bill looked closely at Carl in the dimly lit room. "What happened, Carl?" he asked with a sympathetic tone.

"I was beaten, Bill! I was beaten, and my family has been threatened." The threat to Carl's family was part of the new cover story.

"By who? Why?"

Carl emptied his glass, and Bill immediately refilled it.

"Some men from work. They think I'm a damn Nazi, Bill! I was almost caught trying to get the plans for you, and now they all suspect me as a Nazi supporter! Bill, they threatened to hurt my daughter!" Carl was obviously very upset by now. His voice was rising.

"Carl, calm down. Don't make a scene." Bill's head swiveled examining the room to see if Carl had brought on any attention.

"Bill, I can't do this anymore. I have to protect my daughter. I can't do this!"

Carl emptied his glass and immediately followed with another. Bill noticed the man seated at the table across the room from them who was closely watching their conversation. He also noticed the stealth camera that was capturing their meeting. Carl was completely oblivious of the man.

"Carl, nothing will happen to your family. We can protect you. I'll assign some agents to maintain surveillance on your house and your daughter to assure her safety. Carl, settle down. We'll take care of this for you."

Carl cringed at the thought of this liar professing to protect his family. His total body showed his repulsion, but Bill mistook this for Carl's worried concern for his family. "Like I was protected from the beating I took?!"

"Carl, we were not aware of the men who had this suspicion about you. I am sorry about that. But, just know that it will not happen again. I can assure you of this. You have to trust me, Carl." Bill's tone was calming and reassuring.

Agitated, Carl raised his voice, "You are nothing, and you can't protect my daughter!"

Across the room, the man shifted in his chair concerned that he might have to intervene. He paused as Bill reached across the table and touched Carl on the shoulder to show his feigned care and concern. Carl was repulsed by the touch, but he tried not to show it. He knew that he had to appear to remain loyal to Bill.

Carl hung his head and sighed. "I just need some time, Bill. I just need some time. Can you really protect my daughter?" Carl forced himself to be calm.

"Absolutely, Carl. I'll get it set up and have someone keeping an eye on your home and your daughter by tomorrow."

"I'm not so concerned about myself, Bill, but I need to be sure my daughter is safe. I don't know what these men might do."

"I understand, Carl. Trust me." Bill felt that he finally had Carl's emotions under control.

Carl took another drink. He felt steadier now. He knew Bill could see that he was upset. Bill just didn't know the real reason for Carl's agitation.

"Now, I'm willing to let things settle a bit for you, Carl, but we can't wait too long. I hope you understand. Timing is very important in taking down this network. We're just so close, and, Carl, you are the key to making this a success. Your country needs you for this." He was building Carl back up, and felt pride in the manner that he was able to control Carl. Part of him looked forward to Carl's downfall when this whole thing was over. There was a slight smile on his face as he admired his shrewd deceit.

After a quiet moment, Bill sat up straight in his chair in a gesture to take charge of the situation. "Let's do this, Carl. Settle down at work. Get back into your normal routine as best you can. Let's see each other at the end of the week, Friday night. We can meet at that restaurant on the east side of town and restart this whole thing. How's that sound?"

Carl looked into Bill's eyes as he spoke, "Sure. Okay. I just need to get all of this out of my head for a bit. Yeah, Friday night will be fine."

"Good, Carl. I'll have an agent in place for your daughter by tomorrow. You have nothing to worry about."

Bill got up from his chair. He placed his hand on Carl's shoulder as he started toward the door.

Once Carl knew Bill was gone, he took another drink and slammed the glass down on the table. *That lying bastard!*

An hour later, the man from across the room helped Carl get home. Carl was the FBI agent's only priority.

Chapter 22

Carl struggled his way through the rest of his week at work. He was getting the cold shoulder from everyone. He found himself being excluded from most conversations. His thoughts and ideas were not sought out as they had once been. He thought Mr. Herrington had made it clear that Carl was not in any way a Nazi sympathizer, but there was little change in attitudes among the men.

Carl felt abandoned. It wasn't that he was a very social person to begin with, but Carl was now not only a social outcast but also an outcast from his own tight-knit team of co-workers. His work had always been what defined him. Without the ability to be really focused on the work, Carl was now simply lost.

He finally decided to talk to Mr. Herrington. Having arranged a meeting, Carl went to Mr. Herrington's office.

"Carl, you really shouldn't be coming up here. We don't want anyone getting suspicious. Now, be quick. What do you want?"

Carl was already feeling cast aside by Mr. Herrington just as he had been by his co-workers. "Mr. Herrington, sir, it's just that, well, the guys are still shunning me. I mean, I'm really not able to do my work."

"Carl, I'm sorry. I spoke to Jacob and told him to let the others know that all is good with you . . ."

Carl interrupted, "I know, but can't you do something more?"

"Carl, we just have to wait until this is over. I can't risk arousing any further suspicions. I'm sure you understand. Now, go back to your work area and just stay low. Don't worry about anything."

With that, he showed Carl to the door and ushered him out. Carl shook his head as he made his way down the stairs.

Carl arrived at the restaurant Friday evening, and he saw Bill sitting at a booth near the back of the main room. Carl made his way to the rear of the room winding past the cloth covered tables.

Bill already had a bottle and two glasses waiting. "Carl, good to see you." Bill smiled broadly and gave his hand to Carl.

Carl shook Bill's hand as he sat. "Can we order some dinner?"

"Why sure, Carl, but, here, have a drink first."

Bill filled their glasses. Carl was concerned about drinking too much and saying something he shouldn't, however.

"I think I need some dinner first, Bill," Carl said with a nervous hesitation.

Bill picked up on Carl's uneasiness. "What's wrong, Carl? Have a drink with me."

Bill lifted his glass to Carl urging him to do the same. Carl gave in and drained the glass. Bill immediately filled them and offered up a second glass to Carl. Again, Carl followed suit and poured the liquid down down his throat.

Maybe a drink is exactly what I need. I'll just take it a little easy. "Its just been a rough week, that's all."

"I understand, Carl. Let's relax a bit first. Drink up!"

With several more drinks and Bill's ease, Carl began to relax. Bill saw that Carl was beginning to soften up. It was where he needed Carl to be. He felt good about his ability to manipulate Carl. Carl's drinking problem was one of the reasons he had selected him as the way into Project Rubber Tire in the first place.

Bill had received information that the authorities might be aware of his activities. He arranged to have additional resources brought in to find out what he was up against. He knew Carl was spending some time with executives at the plant. He was also already aware of the amount of security surrounding Carl's work, but he was now aware that the FBI was specifically having conversations with Carl. He needed to soften Carl up and see what he could uncover. Drink was the power that would allow him to get to the bottom of this. So, he continued plying Carl with alcohol.

"So, Carl, tell me about your boss, Mr. Herrington." Bill feigned great interest in Carl's problem at work.

"What do you want to know? He's kind of a . . . let's see, what do they say . . . oh, yeah, he's a pompous ass!" Carl laughed. He did not notice that Bill did not laugh but rather looked more intently into Carl's eyes.

"I thought you got along well with him. Haven't you talked to him a lot lately?"

"Sure, I see Mr. Pompous Ass. He's supposed to be helping me out with those thugs who beat me up, but, ha, yeah, that's a laugh."

"What do you mean, Carl?" Bill intoned with a false interest in Carl's personal needs.

"He won't tell those guys that I'm a good guy! 'Just go back to work, Carl. You understand.' He shuffles me around like I'm a nobody. He never did want me to see Mr. Scholl. I had to insist."

More drinks for Carl.

"Mr. Scholl, the President?"

"Yes, I needed to . . ." Carl realized he was about to say more than he should and stopped mid-sentence.

"You needed to what, Carl?"

"Oh, nothing," Carl replied as he took another drink to keep from saying anything more.

"I understand. Some bosses are a pain in the ass and just don't get what the little guy is going through." Bill appeared to be very understanding.

"Yeah, little guy. That's exactly what he thinks about me."

Across the room behind Carl, the agent sitting in a darkened corner could not hear the conversation because of the noise in the restaurant. He did not like the way that Carl seemed to be agitated, but he could not step in.

"Say, you've probably seen more government agents around the plant, haven't you?" He felt Carl had softened up enough that he could be more direct with his questioning.

"Of course, with what's goin' on and all." Carl was beginning to get confused. Bill was an agent, but the other agents had questioned him, and set up a plan. It was about Bill. But, no, Bill was his friend. Carl just couldn't get his head cleared.

Carl was confused. He was right where Bill wanted him — still talking, but very befuddled. "Tell me about the other agents."

"Well, there was Mr. Smith, and Mr. Jones, and . . . I don't know, one other. They're all gone now. You know them."

"Yeah, sure, I know Smitty and Jonesy. Good agents. Any other guys?"

"Well, there's Agent Jeffers. But, no one knows about him. He's my secret agent . . . a special agent. Shhh."

"Oh, yeah, Jeffers. He's one of the best. What office is he out of now?"

"He's here from Chicago. He likes the small town. I don't think he likes Mr. Herrington anymore than I do. Ha!" Carl rambled.

Carl was now slurring his words. Bill had to pay close attention, but he felt like he was making progress. "Carl, are there any others? Think hard."

"Nope. No others. Just me and Jeffers and Pompous Ass. But, hey, and you, Bill. We probably shouldn't talk about this anymore in public, you know. Hush." Carl placed a finger over his lips.

"You're right, Carl, you're right. How about I give you a ride home?"

Bill helped Carl to his feet and took him outside to the car. The man sitting in the darkened corner of the room followed them at a distance, his hat low to hide his eyes. Although the man tried to be discreet, Bill was aware of him. It was the same man from the last meeting with Carl. With a little support from his contacts, Bill was able to find out who he was.

After getting Carl into the car, Bill watched as the man went to his own car. Bill waited for a moment before starting the engine. He turned on his lights and pulled out of the parking lot. He noticed the car behind him did the same, but maintained some distance between them.

Bill did not drive directly to Carl's house. Carl had already passed out, and Bill wanted to see if the car was following him. After several turns, Bill knew he was right; he was being followed. The driver was good at keeping his distance, but to someone also experienced in tailing a vehicle, Bill had no doubt that he was being followed.

He finally arrived at Carl's house and helped him in the door. There was a light on, but no one was around. He helped Carl to a chair and returned to his car.

The other car was not within sight, but Bill knew he was nearby. Two blocks later, he once again saw the tail.

Now it was Bill's turn. He sped around a corner and cut back two blocks. With his lights off, he was able to move stealthily and eventually pull up behind the car that had been tailing him. He turned on his lights and made it obvious that he was now the one doing the tailing. He loved the control he had.

The car headed to the nearest route leaving town and attempted to outrun Bill's car. It was no use, Bill was keeping up with the other car. After several miles, the lead car appeared to give up, slowed down, and pulled over. Bill pulled up behind the car.

He heard a shout from the front car. "Why are you following me?"

Bill rolled down his window and shouted back, "I can't hear you. What do you want?"

The man opened his door, exited the car, and moved toward Bill's car pretending to be a confused driver. Bill noticed the man had one hand in his pocket, holding a gun. Bill reached inside his coat and removed his own weapon.

The man neared Bill's car and looked down at him. "Why're you followin' me? What d'ya want?" He quickly surveyed the car assuring himself there were no other occupants.

"I think you have it backwards," Bill smirked. "You were following me." Bill smiled broadly at the man.

The man began to straighten himself. "Look, I don't want any trouble. I'll just be on my way."

He did not see the pistol being raised until it was too late. Two shots in quick succession pierced the quiet country night and slammed the man in the chest throwing him to the ground.

Bill opened the door and stepped out. The man was bleeding badly but still breathing. Bill placed another shot directly into the man's head, and he became completely still.

Bill reached inside the man's coat and removed a wallet. Inside was his FBI identification confirming what Bill already knew – FBI Special Agent Thomas Patrick. He kept the wallet and ID to be tossed away later.

Bill put the body back in the other car. He drove to a nearby bridge, and worked the car down the embankment until he was nearly completely under the span. He then positioned the body behind the steering wheel. From just above the river's edge, Bill would be able to send the car down the embankment that led under the bridge. The car would be well-hidden and should remain lost for at least a couple of weeks or more.

He put the car in gear and launched it. It followed the bank down under the bridge and disappeared into the quiet water.

Bill watched and smiled as the slow running river covered the roof of the car.

Bill enjoyed the fresh air and a cigarette as he walked back to his own car. The cool clear night felt good to him and reminded him of the nights of his boyhood home in Germany. As a boy, he would often slip out at night to be away from his abusive father. Alone, lying on the tenement rooftop, he thought about his future, a future in which his father would suffer dearly.

It was three days later when the local newspaper headline announced a tragic collision with a train just outside of town. Mr. Herrington and Special Agent Jeffers were accidentally killed when the car they were riding in failed to stop at a railroad crossing, killing both men instantly.

Chapter 23

Employees at the plant were shocked at the death of Super-intendent Ray Herrington, a longtime employee of Allis-Chalmers. Carl was among the men who were stunned at the death, but he did not waste any time grieving for the man. However, the death of Special Agent Jeffers was a different story for Carl. He had grown to respect the man and appreci-ated his real interest in Carl's personal needs.

Of course, he didn't know where this left him with the plan to expose Bill and the Nazi spy ring. He seemed to have no one to turn to. None of the other FBI agents had yet to contact him. He was fearful of meeting with Bill since he didn't know what to do next.

So, for the next three days, Carl left work quickly and went straight home. By that third day, his daughter made a com-ment to her father about his being home right after his shift at the plant ended. He made the excuse that he had not been feeling well and simply decided to come straight home after work for a few days.

The very next day at work, Carl was summoned to the of-fice of new Superintendent Frank Barnes. Carl heard some of the men talking about the new superintendent who had come from the Allis-Chalmers headquarters in Wisconsin. No one seemed to know anything about him, however. Carl wondered if the FBI had filled him in on their plan. He approached the meeting with a deep sense of uneasiness.

Carl made his way to the second floor and to the door that was still lettered with "Superintendent Herrington." He was told to wait outside the office in a chair and that Superintendent Barnes would call him in shortly.

Carl sat still in the chair wondering what the meeting was all about. He was hoping that the new superintendent would not accuse him of what all the other men were thinking. He wondered if maybe the men had already approached him and laid out their suspicions of Carl. He fidgeted and started to get angry as he sat there waiting.

Then he overheard the new superintendent speaking loudly, apparently on a phone call.

"No, do not call me here again! We will meet at the appointed times and places. We cannot risk even the slightest chance of being caught!"

There was a pause as the other party was likely replying. Then the superintendent spoke again. Carl was now listening intently.

"Good. Now proceed as planned. Arrange another meeting and get this thing back on track. I'll do my part, but you must make him cooperate." Pause. "Yes."

The conversation seemed to cease. Carl sat still. Within moments, a tall, thin blonde man opened the door and asked Carl to come in and sit down. He was a well-dressed and handsome man. He was much younger than Mr. Herrington. This seemed odd to Carl as the executives and bosses always appeared to be older gentlemen.

"Carl, thank you for coming to see me. Let's get right to the point." He sat in the chair behind the desk, but he leaned forward with his hands folded and looked intensely into Carl's eyes. "I've been informed about the problems you've faced at work. I understand that some of the men in the plant continue to be suspicious of you, Carl. Please know that I do not share their suspicions. From all the information that I have reviewed, you were completely cooperative and cleared of any fault whatsoever."

Superintendent Barnes sat upright in his chair. He paused as if waiting for Carl to comment. Carl sat still waiting for Superintendent Barnes to continue.

His hands still folded, the superintendent looked up at the ceiling before continuing to speak. "Carl, I want you to know that I will do everything I can to support you. You are a very valuable member of the team; heck, you're one of the key members of the team. Security has tightened here for obvious reasons, but, Carl, I want you to know that we are relying on you."

There was another long silence before Carl now spoke. "I want to thank you, Mr. Barnes, sir. It means a lot to me to have you say that."

"Well, Carl, I'm sure the situation will not change overnight, but we'll hopefully see things get better for you sooner rather than later. You and I will keep in contact. I think things are going to work out just fine, Carl. I have a feeling you and I have a lot in common. Yes, you will do just fine." Another pause before Superintendent Barnes stood. "That will be all, Carl." He smiled as he ushered Carl out of the office, his hand on Carl's back.

What would Superintendent Barnes and I have in common? That was an odd thing to say.

Carl returned to the project office through the added security that was now in place. He went to the tool room where it seemed he was now relegated to appease the concerns of his co-workers that he might see or hear more than they thought he should.

The next day, as Carl hurried to his car after a long day, he saw Agent Smith and another man waiting at his car. Carl was both pleased and concerned to see Agent Smith.

"Carl, I'm sure you remember me . . . from our, um, 'meeting' at the plant." He reached out his hand to Carl.

Carl shook his hand and replied somberly, "I don't think I could forget that 'meeting.'"

"Just remember, Carl, that the outcome was good for you."

Carl looked at the other man. He was a tall, well-groomed, and good looking man. Just standing there, he seemed to have an air of authority about him. He gave a warm smile to Carl as their eyes met.

"Sorry. Carl, this is Special Agent in Charge Robert Johnson. Bob, this is Carl Schmidt."

The two men exchanged a firm handshake. Agent Johnson quickly assessed Carl from the look in his eyes to his handshake to the way he walked across the parking lot to the way he was standing and to the way he saw Carl assessing him.

"Hello, Carl. I've spent the past week studying the case. Things have obviously taken a more serious turn with the loss of Superintendent Herrington and the two federal agents."

Two agents. What does he mean two agents?

"I'll be taking over your assignment for Special Agent Jeffers. As I'm sure you're aware, Special Agent Jeffers was a fine man. Agent Smith provided me with all of the files from your meeting. We've also done an extensive background work-up on you. So, I hope you don't mind me saying that I feel like I know you already."

"Yes, Agent Jeffers was a very pragmatic man. I'm sorry for his tragic death." Carl paused. "But you said the loss of two agents. I don't understand."

"Carl, we had another agent working deeper undercover on this assignment. He closely monitored Bill Gaines' every move. Unfortunately, he was found murdered."

"Murdered?! Was he here in La Porte? What happened?"

"As I said, he was closely watching Bill Gaines. He actually came to town with Special Agent Jeffers, but, as I said, he was under deeper cover, which is why you never met him. He was with you at every meeting with Gaines."

"Murdered." Carl was in disbelief. "By who? By Gaines? My God!" Carl cautiously looked around to see if anyone else was listening. Fortunately, they were alone.

"We don't know yet who murdered him. It could have been Gaines, or it could have been someone working with Gaines."

"But, are they coming after me next?!" Carl was obviously disturbed. "Or my daughter?!"

Agent Johnson reached out to Carl's shoulders. "No, Carl. You're key to this organization's efforts. They need you. You are completely safe, and we'll have two agents keeping an eye on you and your family at all times. Carl, they can't maintain their efforts to steal the plans from this plant without you. They are just too far along and too committed. In fact, it's because of this that we'll catch them."

"You want me to continue?! I don't know. With everything that's happened . . . I mean, how can I even look at Bill?" The life drained from Carl's face.

"Carl, let's go somewhere where we can talk. Agent Smith will ride with you, and I'll follow. We'll go to a nice quiet place down by the lake."

Without allowing Carl to respond, the men got in their cars and left the parking lot.

Within ten minutes, they were at Poplar Beach Tavern, a small lakeside restaurant that was next to a dock that catered to the boaters on the lake. It was quiet as the boating season was winding down.

Carl wanted a drink. Bob said that would be fine, but he had to limit his drinking so they could be sure Carl was clear about everything. So, Carl tried to slowly sip at his glass, something that was not easy for him to do. He asked for a second as they made their dinner order with the waitress.

Special Agent in Charge Johnson controlled the conversation. "Carl, I know you haven't met with Gaines for over a week. We can use the excuse of the death of your boss to cover that. You can let Gaines know how concerned this made you about continuing to work with him. Then, let him know that you're ready to continue. You can hesitate about it, and let Gaines feel that he has talked you into it. Can you do this?"

Carl nodded as he sipped his whiskey.

Chapter 24

Carl returned to his normal routine and went to the tavern after work the following day. It was an hour later that he was joined by Gaines.

Placing a bottle on the table, Gaines greeted Carl, "Well, Carl, it's good to see you again. Where've you been?"

It sounded more like an interrogation than a friendly question in Carl's mind. Maybe he was just being overly sensitive. He tried to concentrate. "Things have just been a bit nuts at the plant, Bill. You know, with the death of Mr. Herrington and all. And nothing has improved between the other men and me." The downtrodden sound of his voice was real, just not for the reason that he was trying to portray to Bill.

"And, security has been greatly tightened. Bill, I don't know how I'm going to be able to do what you want." Although he was trying to avoid drinking too much, he swallowed the full glass, and Bill immediately refilled it.

"Carl, relax. Actually, I think things are going to get easier for you." He smiled at Carl.

"How so?" Carl was puzzled by his statement.

Bill leaned forward. "We have a new plan that's going to be much easier for you, Carl. I know this has been difficult for you, but Mr. Herrington's untimely death has given us an opening. I know it's an awful thing to think, but Mr. Herrington's death will not have been in vain if we are able to pull this off and put an end to this spy ring."

"I don't know, Bill." Carl was shaking his head. "I don't see how any of this can get easier. The men treat me like I'm going to betray them at any moment. There's no trust, and they're constantly watching me for the slightest wrong move."

Carl was starting to convince himself not to go through with this. Of course Special Agent in Charge Johnson had told him to be hesitant and let Gaines talk him into doing whatever he wanted Carl to do. Now, he hoped he hadn't overplayed his hand and shown too much reluctance.

"Carl, look, I understand, but your country needs your help in this. Just sit tight for a few days. Go about your normal routine. Ignore the men; think about the real good you'll be doing. Carl, this will be much easier this time."

He poured Carl another drink.

"Meet me here Thursday evening. By then, everything should be in place and ready to go."

Nothing changed for Carl over the next couple of days. The situation at work was unchanged. Progress continued on the project, but just a bit slower with less reliance on Carl's abilities. It was obvious to Carl that the new superintendent had said nothing to the men. Or, if he had, they certainly did not heed his words. Carl did not see anything getting easier.

During this time, he had not had any further contact with Agent Johnson. He was following the plan as set forth in their last meeting, but he was allowing doubt to creep in. He felt he was out on a limb all alone.

Wednesday night, Carl got drunk as he hadn't done for several weeks. He passed out in his chair at home under the watchful eye of his mother-in-law and daughter.

Work at the plant on Thursday was no different. If anything, Carl felt as though the men were keeping a closer watch on him. He was feeling the pressure of being watched by everyone no matter where he went. It was becoming unbearable for him.

He hurried to the tavern after work longing for a drink. He arrived prior to Gaines and had several drinks before he was joined at the table. Gaines smiled at Carl as he sat. Usually, Gaines provided a bottle for them, but tonight he sat down empty-handed.

"Good evening, Carl. How was work today?" Again, it felt more like an interrogation than a friendly concern.

Carl was curt, "Same as usual." He emptied the glass in front of him and stared into the bottom.

"Carl, that's good. It means no one is suspecting anything."

Gaines noticed Carl staring into his empty glass. He signaled to the bartender to bring two glasses.

"Carl, it won't be long now. I want to be sure you are completely clear with the next step. Try to keep your mind as sharp as you can."

The bartender set one glass in front of each man. Without looking up, Carl quickly downed the drink.

"Carl, listen carefully. This comes to a conclusion tomorrow. As I said, it will be very easy for you. You won't have to sneak back into the office. In fact, you won't even be around the men when we make the exchange."

"The exchange?" Carl now fixed his eyes on Gaines.

"Carl, we have another man on the inside who will work with you. This is the easy part. The man is going to provide you with an object to pick up. You will merely exit the plant without anyone being suspicious of you. You simply pick it up, go to your car, and meet me at the restaurant. I'll take it from there, and you will be the hero. We'll have these guys!" Gaines sat up straight and smiled victoriously at Carl.

"What am I picking up?"

"We studied several scenarios, but the man will have a set of plans – the fake plans, of course – hidden in the lining of a jacket. He will make sure that you pick up the jacket and carry it out. I told you this would be easy, Carl." Gaines paused to be sure Carl was paying attention.

"Now, just as was previously planned, the contact will be meeting you. I want you to go to the restaurant and sit at a table in the back. Place the coat on the chair next to you. When the contact arrives and picks up the jacket, we'll nab him right then and there. It will be over, Carl. You can have a nice dinner and go home as a hero for your country!"

Gaines smiled encouragingly at Carl and pushed the drink sitting in front of him to Carl. Carl looked at Gaines, then took the drink.

"Do you completely understand, Carl?"

"Yes, I take the jacket from work and bring it to the restaurant. I sit in the back and lay the jacket on the chair." Carl paused and posed a question, "But, how will this man get the jacket to me. Who is he?"

"Carl, just know there will be an opportune time, and you will easily make this happen. Nothing will look out of the ordinary or suspicious. You don't need to know any more than that. Are we good?" He maintained a confident smile at Carl.

Carl knew he had to accept the plan, but maybe he could help the FBI if he knew who would be providing the jacket.

"Sure, we're good. I guess I just thought it might be easier if I knew ahead of time who the man is – you know, to avoid any chance of error."

Carl downed the drink that had been placed before him.

"Don't worry about any of that, Carl. Look, I have to be going. I'll see you at the restaurant tomorrow evening. Okay?"

"Yeah."

Gaines now spoke with a serious tone, "Carl, don't let me down – don't let your country down. Take it easy tonight. Keep your head clear. I'll see you tomorrow, and we'll finish this together."

Gaines stood and left the tavern. Carl sat for several minutes without thinking, merely staring into space. He was aroused when the bartender sat two more glasses in front of him.

The bartender spoke coldly to Carl, "Your friend said I had to cut you off after this. He pays me well, you understand. You can't hang around here tonight."

Carl looked down at the drinks in front of him. He put his fingers around the nearest glass. After a moment, he lifted the glass and quickly swallowed. He immediately picked up the second glass and did the same. Without hesitation, he pushed his chair away from the table and exited the bar. He had a bottle at home that would do.

Chapter 25

Trying his best not to drink too heavily, Carl spent a restless night at home lost in half-awake dreams. He saw himself running from the plant with a large red jacket in his hands. He ran toward his car which seemed to get farther away the faster he raced. Suddenly, he was being chased by three dark-eyed men in black suits. He had to get to his car! But, as he finally approached his car, the three men were now there waiting for him.

He stopped in his tracks, looked about, then ran toward the gates hoping to escape the men. The dash to the gate was not unlike that to the car. Except, now, his legs were growing heavier with each stride forward. The black-suited men were gaining on him. He neared the gate, but, as at the car, the three men were now waiting for him at the gate.

He stopped and looked around him. In addition to the three men at the gate, there were now multiple versions of these men surrounding him and closing in on him. They were all reaching for his jacket. Carl held tightly as they attacked him.

Carl awoke with terror and was soaked in sweat. He was momentarily unsure of his surroundings, but then he realized he was in bed and had had a nightmare. He tried to shake it off, but it all seemed too real.

He looked at the bottle next to his bed. He wrapped his hands around the bottle and tilted it up to drain it into his mouth, but not a drop was left. Carl sat up on the edge of the bed and ran his fingers through his thick, wavy hair.

Carl was still unsure of his ability to handle the situation to the end. He just wanted it all to be over. He just wanted to go back to his normal work routine. He just wanted to simply be The Blacksmith, a role he was comfortable with.

He laid back down in bed hoping to get back to sleep, but the next few hours were a mix of restless sleep and worried wakefulness.

Carl was on edge when he arrived at work, but he had been so to some degree anyway for the past several weeks, so no one took any notice of his demeanor. He felt the same cold stares and unmistakable hatred. He felt tightness in his chest and a twisted emptiness in his stomach.

Passing through security, Carl was ignored by his co-workers, but he could feel them despise him as he had been able to do for some time now. It seemed to bother him more today, however. He was about to help the government break up a German spy ring, yet to the others he was perceived, at best, as a German sympathizer and, at worst, a Nazi. It sickened him. He just wanted to yell and let everyone know the truth . . . but he couldn't. *It will be over by this very night.* He did his best to convince himself that he could get through this.

The day went like every other recent day. He spent his time in the tool room doing menial tasks while the rest of the team wrestled with recent engineering changes. They would not even think about asking Carl to help.

At noon, Carl ate his meager lunch alone sitting on the steps outside of the plant. He did not even finish the little food that he had brought in his lunch pail. He began to wonder when he would be contacted, or how it would take place.

Later, as the end of the day neared, Carl began to wonder if something had gone wrong. No one had approached him. There were no indications from anyone that something involving him was about to take place.

Then the secretary entered the area and told Carl that Superintendent Barnes wanted to see him. *Now what? I don't need this interruption. What if the contact tries to reach me, and I'm in the superintendent's office?*

Carl followed the secretary to the second floor where he had a seat outside the superintendent's office. The lettering on the door had been changed to read "Superintendent Barnes." He listened for any activity. He heard the superintendent speaking, but his voice was too quiet to be heard. It was likely he was on the phone.

Shortly, the conversation ended. Then, Carl heard a buzz as the secretary notified Superintendent Barnes that Carl was waiting outside the office. Immediately, the door opened and Carl was asked to come in.

"Carl, good afternoon! How has your day been?" Superintendent Barnes seemed to be speaking loudly as if trying to talk over some interfering sound.

"Uh, fine, thanks, sir."

Barnes motioned to the chairs in front of his desk, "Have a seat, Carl."

Carl sat in the chair nearest the door.

"I wanted to see how things were going with you and your work. Has there been any improvement in your, uh, situation?"

Again, the volume of his voice was increased. It was not that he was yelling at Carl, he was just speaking very loudly.

"Well, uh, to tell you the truth, nothing has really changed."

"Sorry to hear that, Carl. I guess I'll have to speak with the men again."

Again? Did he ever really say anything to them? "Sure, I guess."

"Look, Carl, things will get better. I think things will be much better for you after today."

Carl was fidgeting a bit. The plant's whistle blew announcing the end of the shift. Carl had not yet met his contact, and he was becoming more uneasy. His right foot tapped the floor.

"Carl, try to relax. Go home and get a good night's rest. You'll see, tomorrow will be better."

Superintendent Barnes rose from his chair behind his desk signaling that it was time for Carl to leave. Carl stood as well, took two steps toward the door, and reached for the door handle.

"Carl."

With his hand on the doorknob Carl turned to look at Superintendent Barnes.

"Don't forget your jacket." Superintendent Barnes pointed to a chair at a small conference table in the back of the room. There on the chair was a well-worn simple work jacket.

Carl's face went ashen. He looked at the jacket. *Superintendent Barnes?!*

The superintendent smiled as his hand continued to point at the jacket. Carl slowly let go of the door handle. His legs felt like lead as he moved to the chair and picked up the coat. He looked at Superintendent Barnes who was still smiling.

"Just head to the front office entrance. You won't have any problems leaving through there. Have a nice supper, Carl." He was still smiling as Carl exited the office.

By the time Carl reached his car, he was covered in sweat. He couldn't believe that the new superintendent was involved. *Who else is in on this? How many are there? What do I do now?*

Carl sat in his car shaking. Carl had some time before he was to meet Gaines at the restaurant. He needed a drink. He was aware enough to realize he ought to avoid his normal watering holes. He drove to a small bar about halfway to the restaurant and went in for a drink.

He downed two drinks quickly, and the bartender was pouring his third when Special Agent in Charge Johnson sat on the stool next to him. Carl was startled as Agent Johnson sat down. He finished the third drink.

"Carl, take it easy. You did fine."

"But, it was the new superintendent!" Carl said in a loud whisper.

"We know, Carl. We've known for some time. He was placed there by the foreign agents from Wisconsin. The organization is large, and this is the break we needed to bring it down. We're almost there, Carl. You have to put that coat in Gaines' hands at the restaurant. Then we'll have them with the goods, and this will all be over."

"Sorry, I'm just confused and frightened by all of this!"

Carl signaled the bartender for another drink. Agent Johnson watched as Carl finished the glass. He then reached out and placed his right hand over the empty glass.

"Breathe deep, Carl. Now, you'll meet Gaines at the restaurant. We're quite sure that Barnes will be there as well. It'll be okay if you're surprised by his presence. Just don't make a scene. We don't want anything to spook them. Okay, Carl?"

"Sure. I'll be fine. I just needed a drink to settle my nerves. I'll be fine." Carl was trying to convince himself as much as he was trying to convince Agent Johnson.

"We'll have several men inside the restaurant. You'll be safe at all times, Carl. Just carry the coat in and set it next to you. As soon as Gaines picks it up, my agents will move in and arrest the men. Carl, it will be over. We'll have them, and you can get back to a normal life. Carl, look at me."

Carl turned his head and looked at Agent Johnson. He was able to see the confidence in his eyes. Carl truly felt like this man had his back. *I can do this.*

Agent Johnson reached out his hand to Carl. The two men shook hands and smiled. Agent Johnson paid for the drinks, and the men left the small pub.

Chapter 26

Carl arrived at the restaurant, but he did not see Gaines anywhere. When he was asked if he wanted to be seated, Carl said that, yes, he would like a table in the back, and he would wait there for the others who should be arriving soon.

Carl sat in a chair facing the entrance so that he would be able to see Gaines when he arrived. He fidgeted for a bit then waved the waiter over and ordered a drink – a double. The waiter politely took his order and returned shortly with the drink. Carl was trying his hardest to drink slowly. He just needed to hold the glass in his hands. It helped him to relax.

He wondered if Gaines might not be watching him to make sure he was alone. Carl had not seen Agent Johnson enter either. He wondered which of the other men in the restaurant were agents. He looked carefully at those who did not have their back to him, but there was nothing that indicated to him which men might be agents. Most of the men were dressed similarly in suit coats. Carl realized that he was the one who stuck out like a sore thumb.

He had placed the coat on the chair next to him hoping that Gaines would sit there and pick it up right away. Then the agents could swoop in and end this thing.

Carl thought he could hear the clock on the wall across the room ticking as the time crawled on. After several minutes, he saw Gaines enter the room. He slowly scanned the room twice before walking over to Carl.

He approached with a bit of nervousness of his own. It was not something he had previously seen in Gaines. He sat across from Carl, thus avoiding the coat on the chair. He was obviously alone. *Is Barnes coming or not?* Certainly it wasn't a question Carl could ask.

"Carl, I hope your day was productive at the plant."

Gaines held up his hand and ordered a bottle from the waiter. He returned shortly, and Gaines gave his approval to the brand.

"You're awfully quiet, Carl. Tell me about your day."

Carl spoke under his breath. "It was nerve-wracking. I waited all day to find out what I was supposed to pick up! I didn't know it would be Mr. . . ."

Gaines cut him off, "Carl, it was best not to give you too much information. Yes, I'm sure it was a bit of a surprise to you."

"A bit of a surprise! I was shocked. How deep are you, uh, I mean, these guys in to the company?!" Carl hoped his mistake would be ignored by Gaines as only part of Carl's nervousness.

Gaines stared deeply at Carl. "Carl, this is a big deal, bigger than you can imagine. Yes, this organization is deep. Deep not only into this company but into many large manufacturers across the country. Trust me, Carl, this is a very good thing you are doing."

"Well, there's your item sitting on the chair." Carl looked at the jacket on the chair next to him.

"I see. Well done. As soon as Barnes gets here, we'll wrap this up."

Carl finished his drink, and, in his usual manner, Gaines poured him another.

"Barnes is coming?"

"Yes, he'll take the coat, and we'll have him. You can leave here a hero, Carl."

Carl finished another drink and saw Barnes enter the room. *I sure hope the agents are ready to move.*

Barnes came to the table and sat in the other open chair leaving the jacket untouched. Gaines and Barnes exchanged polite hellos, and Barnes simply nodded to Carl.

Barnes leaned over to Gaines and whispered a short comment into his ear. Carl was unable to hear what was said. Gaines merely nodded at the whisper.

Gaines then looked intently at Carl. In a menacing order, he said to Carl, "Pick up the coat. We're leaving."

Gaines placed some bills on the table as Carl looked around the room waiting for someone to move in. *Where are they?*

He had apparently hesitated too long as Gaines broke in, "Move. Now, Carl! And grab your coat." Gaines' head nodded to the jacket on the chair.

Carl reached over and picked up the coat. Gaines motioned him to lead the way to the door. Carl looked about as he walked, but he saw no one paying any attention to the three men.

When they were clear of the entrance, Gaines pushed Carl along to a large black sedan.

"Get in back, Carl."

Carl entered the car. Gaines forced Carl to slide across the seat as he got in beside him. Barnes got into the driver's seat and turned over the engine.

Inside the restaurant, three men rose from their seats and quickly headed for the exit. But, they were cautious about exiting too soon so as not to arouse the suspicion of Gaines and Barnes.

One of the men exited first examining the situation as he entered the parking lot. He saw the doors close on a large black sedan not far away. He walked without hesitating to his car at the rear of the lot. As he did so, the lights of the black sedan came on, and it left the parking lot.

Having been waiting in the parking lot, Special Agent in Charge Johnson pulled up to the first agent who was shortly joined by the two others.

"Well, we weren't expecting this. We'll follow them, carefully swapping the tail between our two cars. Just be cautious and maintain a good distance."

At that, with two agents in each car, they slowly exited the parking lot maintaining a cautious tail on the large black sedan.

Chapter 27

Tailing the sedan west through downtown was easy for the federal agents. The town's Friday night traffic allowed the agents to easily hide their presence. They were trained and experienced in surveillance techniques, and this was just business as usual for them.

What concerned them, however, was what was happening with Carl. He would certainly not have been prepared for something like this to happen. None of them were, but the agents were more easily adaptable to such circumstances.

The FBI was aware of the recent entry of Franz Braun, or Frank Barnes as he was known at Allis-Chalmers, into the case. He was a practical man with very good skills at interrogating individuals. From what the FBI knew about him, he was unlikely to be a problem for Carl at this time.

Gaines, or Wilhelm Gegner, his real name, was a different story. He was a sociopath who saw pleasure in the pain and suffering of others. There was no doubt that he had killed Herrington and Special Agents Jeffers and Patrick. He was the real concern when it came to Carl's safety.

Agent Johnson hoped that Carl could remain calm enough to maintain his role and not let on that he was working with the FBI. He feared that Gegner would quickly eliminate Carl if he knew the truth.

In the black sedan, Carl was trying to keep his head clear. He wanted to believe that the agents were following them, but he had difficulty convincing himself of this.

"Bill, what the heck is going on? Why did we leave so suddenly?" Carl did all he could to sound calm, merely questioning the change in plans.

"Well, Carl, it appears there are some other matters that we need to deal with before we can conclude our business."

"But, you have what you need. Can't you just drop me off and make your move on the spies?" Carl continued to maintain the cover story.

"It's not that simple. Just be patient, Carl. We were about to be overwhelmed by their organization. We were compromised. We're just changing the plan a bit. It'll all be over soon. Trust me."

"Sure, Bill." For now Carl felt he must be safe as long as he continued to play along.

"Frank, head for the farmhouse."

Frank never responded to Bill, he just moved his head slightly and nodded in the rearview mirror.

They continued through town, and Carl thought that surely at any moment the car would be intercepted by the FBI agents. He was cautious, however, not to look around for something to happen. He tried to remain calm, but he sure could use a drink.

As if reading his mind, Bill removed a pint of whiskey from his coat and offered it to Carl. "Go ahead, Carl, we'll be in the car for a bit yet."

Carl took the bottle and had a long draft from it. He followed with another.

The tailing cars kept in communications with their in-car radios. Based on the latest intelligence information, Agent Johnson only knew that they had a hide-out outside of town. They continued following the car west through town. Leaving the business district behind, they now continued past rows of homes. The cars dropped back even further and alternated with one car dropping away then catching up along a parallel route. So far, it did not appear as though the car ahead of them was aware of the tail.

"Are we being followed?" Gaines inquired of Barnes.

"Maybe. I'll know in a moment."

There was a pause as neither man spoke. Meanwhile, Carl emptied the pint that Gaines had given him.

"Oh, yeah, they're on us. They're good, but there are only two cars, and they can only hide that for so long." Barnes spoke with authority of one who knew what he was talking about.

"Pick it up a bit as we get onto the rural back roads."

In the tailing cars, Agent Johnson told the drivers to fall back even farther as the lead car turned south onto a country road. "It'll be too easy for them to spot us out here. Drop way back. Be sure not to lose them, though."

"They're dropping back. They know we can spot them out here on an empty road." Carl saw Barnes smile through the rearview mirror.

"Good. As soon as we top that hill, gun the engine and get us there before they can figure out where we are. Shut off the lights just as soon as you can."

Gaines looked over at Carl whose chin was near his chest as his head bobbed slightly up and down. He was feeling good from the effects of the alcohol. That should make things easier for Gaines.

Over the top of the next hill, Barnes gunned the engine and the car quickly hit top speed on the country road. When he knew he was nearing the farmhouse, he turned off the lights and slowed down. He soon saw the old mailbox leaning into the road. He slammed the brakes and slid the car sideways into the weed-covered dirt driveway.

Carl was roused by the rough ride, and his head popped up in time to see two men throwing open doors to a barn. The car entered and slid to a stop as the barn doors were quickly closed behind them.

The first of the tailing cars rounded the top of the hill and was surprised to no longer see any taillights.

"Bob, we've lost them!" he shouted into the radio. "I don't see any taillights."

The radio squawked, "Look for a side road. We can't lose them. We're coming up on you as fast as we can. Take the first road you see to the right. We'll take the left. If you don't see them quickly get back on this road. We've got to find them!"

"Okay. We should be coming up on the next country mile section shortly." He was quiet. "Yeah, here it is. We're going right!"

"I see your taillights now. We'll go left. Keep your eyes peeled."

The two cars sped away from the road they had been on as they searched for the black sedan in the night, one heading west and one heading east in the dark of the night.

Carl sat still in the car as Gaines and Barnes got out. They were gladly welcomed by the men who had been waiting in the barn. They spoke briefly among themselves, then Gaines approached the car and ordered Carl out.

The tail Barnes picked up on must be the FBI agents. That means they'll be here soon. I just need to remain calm.

Gaines grabbed Carl's arm and pulled him out of the car. He then reached in and picked up the coat. He pushed Carl to one of the other two men who tightly grabbed Carl.

"Bill, what's going on here?"

"Carl, I think you know what's going on. You can drop the act. We know that you met with the FBI after our last meeting. Carl, if you would've just left them out of this and not told them anything, it would've been much easier for you."

"Oh, it was well before our last meeting that they were involved." Carl was feeling brave now, sure that the FBI would enter at any moment. "It was right after I was beaten . . . beaten by the people I work with. People who trusted me, and people who I trusted in turn."

Gaines laughed at Carl. "Trust. Yeah, that is a laugh. You were too stupid to trust in the Home Country, the country of your ancestors. But, no, you and your father before you were traitors to Germany! You must have some Jew blood running through your veins!" Gaines spat on the ground at Carl's feet.

"This is my country! But you, you and your Nazi friends here had to murder two good people – maybe more for all I know. Yes, the FBI asked me to remain in place so they could catch you! I gladly did so, and I would do it again!"

As Carl held his head high, Gaines slapped him then quickly backhanded him causing Carl to stumble and fall.

"A fall-down drunk, that's what you are, Carl, and you will never be anything more. Do you know how I know that, Carl? I know it because your pitiful little life will end tonight! You realize the loss of a drunk in a suicide will not arouse the least bit of suspicion from anyone."

Carl rose to his feet, his hand on his jaw. "Tell me, Bill, what's your real name, the German name you must be so proud of? And, did you really help my family on the *Gellert*, or was that a lie too?"

Again, Gaines laughed, only harder, louder, and longer this time. "My name is Wilhelm Gegner, a name I am proud to have, a name I will no longer have to hide. And, yes, Carl, I was on that ship with you and your family. And, yes, I was there when your family was attacked. I remember the scared little boy who whined for his father. He was a weakling, not worthy of his German heritage. You see, it was my gang that attacked your family! I beat your father; I took his money!" With a wild look in his eyes, Gaines – Gegner – laughed all the more.

Carl lunged at him, but he was slow and unsteady from the effects of the alcohol, and he missed Gaines as one of the other men shoved him to the ground and laughed. He made Carl stay down on his knees with a gun now pointed at his head.

"You're no better now then you were then! You're still a scared little boy, Carl."

All the men now laughed at Carl and called him a traitorous drunk.

"Look what you've done, Carl. You, the one who loves this land so much, you've betrayed your country! You're now really nothing! America no longer wants you, and the Nazi Party doesn't want a weak traitor like you, either! Yes, you must have Jew blood!" The sick laughter continued.

Carl, on his knees, threw his hands and head to the ground crying loudly. "What have I done?!"

Gaines picked up the coat containing the stolen plans. "Indeed, Carl."

Gaines made his way to a light blue coupe next to the black sedan giving more orders, "Take him out back and shoot him. You can put his body in a car and burn it."

Two of the men lifted Carl off the barn floor by his arms and dragged him through a door at the rear of the barn. Shortly thereafter, two gun shots echoed through the country air.

Chapter 28

Gegner smiled that broad victorious smile as he reached the door of the blue coupe. He was full of ruthless pride at having pulled off a great victory for himself and, of course, for the Nazi Party. He had absolutely no bit of empathy for Carl, or for anyone he had killed, for that matter.

As Gegner reached for the door handle, a voice emerged from a dark corner at the back of the barn, "Hold it right there, Wilhelm!"

Gegner stopped and turned around to see a figure moving forward into the dim light of the barn. "Well, well, you must be the revered Federal Bureau of Investigation," he taunted. "You might want to know that you are outnumbered. Perhaps you should drop your weapon and join your friend outside." He had the usual vile smile on his face feeling he had the upper hand in the situation.

"I don't think so, Wilhelm. I didn't hesitate forty years ago, and I won't be backing down now."

"Forty years ago?" Gegner looked puzzled as the smile left his face.

"Aboard the *Gellert*. You know, when you attacked Carl's family." Johnson's gun was steadily aimed on Gegner as he also closely watched Braun.

"Franz, why don't you move over by your slimy friend." He waved the gun to indicate where he wanted Braun to move. "Right there will do." The two Nazis were near enough for

Johnson to cover them, but far enough apart so they could not make a surprise move on Johnson.

A sudden look of realization came over Gegner's face. "That was you?" He laughed aloud. "I should have finished you then." More laughing. "But, I'll be leaving now. I'm sorry you won't be completing your assignment, but you will have an attempted heroic end to your life." The evil smile returned to his face. "I'm sure your Federal Bureau of Investigation will honor you gloriously for almost taking down a Nazi spy ring in America." More sickening laughter.

"No, Wilhelm! Drop the coat, and place your hands on the hood of the car."

"I can't do that. Besides, there's only one of you and four of us. Perhaps you had other agents outside, but they'll likely be joining Carl shortly." He loved the total control he had over the situation.

"No, there are only the two of you." Carl entered the rear door through which the men had escorted him moments ago. "And, you're surrounded by FBI agents."

Wilhelm turned as several other men entered the barn through the rear door as well as the front door. At the rear, the two men who had escorted Carl outside were in handcuffs.

Wilhelm looked around and spoke directly to Agent Johnson who was staring down the gun barrel at Gegner, "You know I can't surrender."

He dropped the jacket and swiftly reached for the pistol in his own coat. A shot rang out, and Wilhelm dropped to the barn floor, his right knee blown apart by the well-placed shot from Agent Johnson. In a pain that he refused to acknowledge, Wilhelm Gegner surrendered, raising his hands far above his head.

There were six FBI agents who rounded up the four German spies. The barn doors were opened and the lights from three cars were turned on to illuminate the scene.

On the dirt floor of the barn, Wilhelm began to writhe in pain he could no longer ignore. One of the agents attended to him, ensuring that the bleeding was under control. The other three men were taken to two of the cars which left swiftly in the night.

"We have an ambulance on the way for you, Wilhelm. We'll get you fixed up so we can take you to a very nice interrogation facility." It was now Agent Johnson's turn to smile, except his smile was one of victory for a job well-done, and done with the safety of everyone assured.

Carl approached Agent Johnson who reached out with his left hand to retrieve the jacket. It was then that Carl noticed the missing finger. Carl's mind quickly flashed back to that moment when his family was befriended upon arriving in America. He clearly saw the young man's missing finger as he picked up his bag.

"Your finger, your missing finger. I remember that! You placed money in my hand, but it was the next day when you picked up your bag, I saw you were missing a finger!"

Robert held up his left hand and looked at it. "A farm accident when I was young."

"I heard what you said to Gaines, er, Gegner. You really were the one who helped my family when I was a child!" Carl looked gratefully into Agent Johnson's eyes. "Well, thank you twice for being there."

"You're welcome. Yes, Carl, that was really me. I was quite surprised when I took over the case and the background on you revealed that to me. It sure took me back when I saw you had come over on the *Gellert* on that voyage that I was on as well."

"A German-American FBI agent! You must have changed your name along the way as well. Robert Johnson isn't even close to German."

"Carl, like so many, our family name was changed when we immigrated to America. Actually, Robert is my true given name, but my family name was Johannes.

Carl extended his hand, "Robert Johannes, it is a real pleasure to meet you. I'm Karl Schmiedemeister, son of Ludwig Schmiedemeister."

They shook hands firmly and clapped each other on the shoulder. As the two men walked through the open barn doors, the sky was lightened by the sun still well below the horizon. In the quiet early morning, they heard the sound of the approaching ambulance in the distance.

Chapter 29

In addition to the four men arrested at the barn, one other man in an upper-level position at Allis-Chalmers in Wisconsin was also arrested.

The German espionage effort on U.S. soil was brought to an end when the local arrests were tied to a much larger ring. There were thirty-three Nazi spies operating mainly on the east cost, but also into the Midwest. The ringleader was Fritz Duquesne, a veteran spy whose efforts focused on U.S. industrial plants. Duquesne himself operated out of Delaware.

The arrests in the Midwest provided the final pieces of evidence to tie the thirty-three spies together and ultimately lead to their arrests. As America entered World War II, it did so with confidence, having broken the major German espionage network hidden in the U.S.

Of the thirty-three spies charged, sixteen pleaded guilty, while the others went to trial. Thirty-two of the thirty-three members of the Nazi spy ring were convicted and sentenced to serve a total of 300 years in prison. The leader of the ring, Duquesne, was sentenced to eighteen years in prison.

Of all of the cases against the spies, Wilhelm Gegner's was the only case that resulted in a murder conviction – a triple murder conviction. Gegner was found guilty for the murders of Raymond Herrington of the Allis-Chalmers Company and FBI Special Agents Al Jeffers and Thomas Patrick. Three weeks following his conviction, Gegner was executed by electric chair in New York.

Carl was welcomed back at the La Porte Allis-Chalmers plant where he was hailed as a hero. There were plenty of pats on the back and apologies from his co-workers. His renewed involvement in the project for the war effort resulted in a new tank with a new form of light-weight, heavy-duty armament being deployed earlier in the war effort than had been anticipated, a real advantage for the soldiers on the European front lines.

Special Agent in Charge Johnson met with Carl to wrap-up all the details of the events and complete his report. Carl was able to provide more detail than he had expected.

As they completed the interviews, Agent Johnson asked Carl if he could speak to him aside from the events of the spy ring. Carl sensed a seriousness to Agent Johnson's tone.

"Carl, I personally respect what you've done. It took a man with a strong character to face, and overcome, the real challenges you had thrown at you. Carl, I can't stress enough that you do have a strong character, a really strong character.

"I want to tell you about someone else who has a strong character. And, Carl, if you'll permit me to get personal, like you, he also has a drinking problem."

Carl stirred nervously, wanting to say something but not knowing what to say, wanting to agree, but not wanting to face the reality in front of Agent Johnson. He simply waited for Agent Johnson to continue.

"Carl, I wouldn't be telling you this if I didn't think you needed help, and if I didn't think there was hope for you to overcome this."

Carl felt like he had to speak. "Look, Bob, I hear what you're saying, and I appreciate your words. Yeah, I've always drank a little too much, but I have stopped at times. In fact, early in Prohibition, I quit for awhile. I can stop. I just need things to settle down a bit."

"Carl, I've heard this story. I've heard it many times. My brother is an alcoholic."

Carl cringed at the word. "Well, alcoholic is a bit strong, Bob. I just drink once in a while after working hard. Or, you've seen the tense situation I've been in for months. A drink just helps relax me . . ."

"Carl, listen to yourself. You're making excuses. That's exactly what my brother did for years. Carl, he hit rock bottom and ended up in jail. Now, I'm not saying that will happen to you, but, Carl, I've seen you express the love you have for your daughter. Get sober and get to really know her. And, let her get to know the real Carl Schmidt, the real father that she knows is in there."

Carl knew Agent Johnson was right. He put his head in his hands and sobbed. "Bob, I don't know what to do! I don't know what to do."

Bob reached out and grabbed Carl's shoulders. "Carl, there is a way out. There is hope. There is a way that this can work. Let me tell you about it.

"There were these two men, Bob and Bill, one from Ohio, and one from New York. Both men were alcoholics, and they were far worse off than you, Carl. They met each other and found help in talking to another man with a drinking problem. They shared this with other men, and they created an organization they call Alcoholics Anonymous, or AA as it is known. Men in need of help get together to provide support for each other. They only use their first names, so no one ever knows who you are unless you want them to know. Carl, this is the real thing. There are nearly 6,000 AA members in almost 150 cities around the country."

Carl was listening intently.

"They have what they refer to as a twelve-step program to guide them through their sobriety. I was able to get my brother involved with a group in Indianapolis. Carl, he has not had a drink in over three years. He's holding down a good job and developing relationships he never thought possible. Carl, this really works. It can, no, it will work for you."

Carl cleared his eyes. "Oh, Bob, I want this. I want to know my daughter. I want her to know me. I want to stay sober. Help me, Bob."

Through his brother, Bob was able to establish a small Alcoholics Anonymous support group in La Porte. Bob's brother was excited to share his path to sobriety in this manner.

Carl returned to his quiet demeanor and solid work ethic. While the men at the plant wanted to buy Carl drinks after work, he was now six weeks sober thanks to the Alcoholics Anonymous organization. It wasn't long before the men were doing all they could to support him on his road to sobriety.

Carl went home each evening after his day at the plant and worked intently on forming anew the relationships with his mother-in-law, his daughter Leona at home, and his two other married daughters. Things were still bumpy with his mother-in-law, but Carl and Leona were making up for a lot of lost time.

Fact and Fiction

The Backdrop of the Historical Novel

In my previous novel, *Hill of the Bear*, I spoke of the fun of writing a historical novel. I noted how the facts of history provide a springboard from which to launch the overall story as well as to develop specific scenes.

In the case of *The Blacksmith*, there are several overarching historical backdrops to the story. These multiple backdrops help provide the scenery as a real backdrop in a theater might. In this case, it was a special pleasure to add some of the history of my childhood hometown of La Porte, Indiana.

The first backdrop is that of immigration in the late nineteenth century. It was not an easy passage for the poorer immigrants. The few scenes in the story were well-researched to provide a look at the challenges presented to immigrants at that time.

As La Porte, Indiana, becomes the location for the story, a bit of the history of the Rumely Company was a must. The Rumely family was responsible for much of the success of the city of La Porte.

Of course, Allis-Chalmers became huge in La Porte for quite a number of years until its final closing in 1985. They purchased Advance-Rumely during the Great Depression and had an extensive agricultural business.

Because of the timing of the story, there is a modest mention of the Great Depression and Prohibition. Prohibition is brought in because of our main character's drinking problem. This was opportune to presenting the story of Alcoholics Anonymous.

Finally, there is the German spy ring that is an integral part of the story. Yes, there were German spies in the United States just prior to our entry into World War II. The Duquesne Spy Ring, consisting of thirty-three spies operating in the United States, was woven into the story to provide our antagonists.

The main character of the story, Carl Schmidt (Karl Schmiedemeister) was inspired by my maternal grandfather,

Robert C. Wendt, about 1944

Robert C. Wendt. My grandfather immigrated to America in April of 1882 at the age of three aboard the actual passenger steamer *S. S. Gellert*. The young family consisted of 31-year-old Ludwig Wendt, a farmer, his 29-year-old wife Johanna, son Robert, age 3, and two babies, Ernst and Martha, from Ganschendorf, Pomerania (Germany).

Robert Wendt worked as a blacksmith, and he was actually the last working blacksmith at the Allis-Chalmers plant in

La Porte. He also shared one trait with our story's main character – my grandfather was an alcoholic.

Robert Wendt, much like Carl Schmidt, was divorced by his wife, Bertha. At the time she left him, about 1927, Robert had two daughters still at home, my mother Shirley, born in 1924, and her sister Marjorie, born in 1917. In all, there were eight children born to Robert and Bertha. All similarities to the characters of our story end there.

Chapter 1. A substantial amount of research was undertaken to provide an accurate picture of immigration as it would have happened in 1900. Actually, it was improving to some degree by that time. Steerage, however, was an unpleasant experience for the poorer immigrants crammed into the lower hold of the ship, basically the cargo hold.

The *S. S. Gellert* was a real ship used for immigration and was first launched in 1874. In 1881, a second boiler was added (see second stack in the photo below). It was decommissioned and broken up for scrap at Hamburg, Germany, in 1896, prior to the time it is used for this story.

The story of the attack on the Schmiedemeister family is fictional. (By the way, "Schmiedemeister" translates to "master blacksmith.")

S. S. Gellert, after 1881

Chapter 2. Most of us think of the arrival of early immigrants at Ellis Island. Ellis Island opened on January 1, 1892. From 1850 to 1890, immigrant processing was done at a center called the Castle Garden located at the southwest tip of Manhattan. After a rift between New York and the federal government, beginning in 1890, immigrants were processed at the Barge Office, located at the southeast foot of Manhattan. The new facility on Ellis Island that opened in 1892 was a three-story wooden structure designed to handle up to 10,000 immigrants per day.

Just before midnight on June 14, 1897, a fire broke out burning the structure on Ellis Island to the ground. Unfortunately, all administrative records from 1855 to 1890 were lost.

So, on June 14, 1897, the Barge Office was once again set up as the processing center for immigrants. It was another three-and-a-half years before the Ellis Island processing center was rebuilt, opening on December 17, 1900.

Arriving in America in April of 1900, the Schmiedemeister family was processed through the Barge Office at the tip of Manhattan.

Chapter 3. This chapter of Karl's encounter with Christiana is fiction. I did, however, incorporate the name of one of my great-grandfathers, Friedrich Schirmeyer. He was the father of Robert Wendt's wife, Bertha. It's fun to use family names in the story.

One small bit of historical fact is the mention of Guenther Brothers Brewery, a real brewery in La Porte at the time of the novel.

Chapter 4. This chapter introduces some of the La Porte history contained in the book. First is the blacksmith business. Two firms are mentioned, Wegner's and Pitner's. Both were real blacksmith businesses in La Porte, and Mr. Wegner did apprentice for Mr. Pitner. The quoted motto of Wegner's company is actual.

I also used the name Fred Bluhm for one of the characters after finding mention of him as a blacksmith in Kingsbury, Indiana. (My paternal 3Xgreat-grandfather Ira Barber also happened to be a blacksmith from Kingsbury.)

A second historical reference introduces the Rumely Company. Some of the history of the company is given in the next chapter. Suffice it to say that the Rumely Company, as well as the Rumely family itself, had a major impact on the city of La Porte, and beyond. In more recent history, for example, A. J. Rumely was elected to serve as the mayor of La Porte in 1979. He was the grandson of Meinrad Rumely, the founder of the Rumely Company. A. J. Rumely was also the president of the La Porte Foundry, a company his father, A. J. Rumely Sr., started 75 years before it closed in 1990.

Chapter 5. A snapshot of the history of the founding of the Rumely Company is given in this chapter. There is no relationship to any actual events in the remainder of the chapter.

Chapter 6. This chapter is all fictitious.

Chapter 7. At the beginning of the chapter is a further bit of history of the Rumely Company as it becomes the Advance-Rumely Company through acquisitions.

This chapter brings in some of the realities that those of German heritage faced at the outbreak of World War I. The description of the anti-German sentiment is real. It is likely – and I did not see anything to the contrary – that with the German population of La Porte and the position of the Rumely Company, that the Germans were not treated as badly as they were in larger cities. The description of men terrorizing the German neighborhood is fiction.

The registration of Germans as alien enemies was an actual program. I have my grandfather Robert Wendt's registration dated February 22, 1918. It is a small four-page pamphlet containing his photo, fingerprint, address, and signature. Robert apparently made a trip to Chicago on September 23, 1918. There is an entry on a page entitled "INDORSEMENTS" which reads, "This permits Mr. Robert C. Wendt to visit Chicago Hammond and Gary several days." It is signed by Alfred Norris, Chief of Police.

The inside cover denotes the penalty for not carrying the card at all times: "An alien enemy required to register shall not, after the date fixed for his registration and the issuance to him of a registration card, be found within the limits of the United States, its territories or possessions, without having his registration card on his person under liability, among other penalties, to arrest and detention for the period of the war."

Robert C. Wendt: U.S. Alien Enemy
Registration Photo, 1918

Chapter 8. The nonfiction element of this chapter is the character of Milwaukee police chief John Janssen. He was credited with eliminating a lot of corruption in the Milwaukee department. Robert Johnson and his exploits are fiction.

Chapter 9. This chapter is fiction. However, I did use the date that my grandfather Robert C. Wendt became a naturalized citizen of the U.S. as the date that Carl became a citizen.

Chapter 10. The financial collapse of the Great Depression, beginning in 1929 and carrying on through the 1930s, took its toll on the Advance-Rumely Company. As early as January 1930, the company's management began seeking a buyer for the company. Talks with the Allis-Chalmers Manufacturing Company proved fruitful, and by May 1931, Allis-Chalmers agreed to take over the firm.

Chapter 11. The emergence of Hitler as the Chancellor of Germany and the subsequent events noted are the historical record. The personal events of Wilhelm Gegner are fiction.

Chapter 12. The stories of Dr. Robert Smith and William Wilson are true. This is an actual account of the manner in which the Alcoholics Anonymous organization came into existence.

Chapter 13. The development of the *Abwehr* and the German intelligence organizations is true. Germany was concerned about the potential support of Great Britain by the United States as war neared, and a network of spies was cultivated.

Chapter 14. There is a good mix of fact and fiction in this chapter. While the War Department did work with many manufacturers during the war, there was no secret program with Allis-Chalmers. The discussion of tank designs for World War II, however, is real. Weight and speed were key challenges.

There was no known meeting with Allis-Chalmers, but I did use the name of the president of the company at that time, Max Babb. In reality, the Allis-Chalmers Company did work on projects for the war effort at multiple locations around the country. Products included anti-aircraft guns, propeller shafts for destroyers, cruisers and submarines, slides for 16-inch naval guns, aircraft turbo superchargers, snow trailers, and at least 11,249 tractors of various types. (http://usautoindustry-worldwartwo.com/allis-chalmers.htm.)

On April 6, 1944, it was announced that the La Porte Plant would begin production of the M6 High Speed Tractor. The Allis-Chalmers La Porte Plant built 1,235 of these 38-ton tractors in 1944-45. (http://usautoindustryworldwartwo.com/allis-chalmers.htm.) So, there was no development of a new tank by the company, and the actual production in La Porte took place later in the war.

While Carl develops an idea for a composite armor plating, in reality, the earliest known composite armor for armored vehicles was developed as part of the U.S. Army's T95 experimental series from the mid-1950s.

The story makes note of using a Model HD14 tractor chassis for the new tank. The La Porte Plant did actually produce this tractor about this time. Also, the GM 6-71 engine, and its twin configuration designated 6046, were engines used in tanks.

Finally, the military assigned "M" numbers to their vehicles. Consecutive "Motor Carriages" begin with the designation M1 and increase to M56. The list I uncovered indicated that M11 was unused, so that became the designation for the Allis-Chalmers tank of the story.

Chapter 15. As mentioned in the notes for the previous chapter, the earliest known composite armor for armored vehicles was developed in the mid-1950s. Those early composites used fused silica glass between the steel sheets. Later composites used ceramic materials.

Chapter 16. The Nazi spy ring under the leadership of Frederick "Fritz" Duquesne did actually infiltrate the United

States prior to the U.S. entry into World War II. By December 13, 1941, every member of the group had either pleaded guilty or been convicted at trial. On January 2, 1942, the thirty-three members of the ring were sentenced to serve a total of over 300 years in prison.

Duquesne was actually a South African who came to the U.S. in 1902 and became a citizen in 1913. On one occasion he did secure material on a new type of bomb from the DuPont plant in Wilmington, Delaware.

Besides Duquesne, one other actual spy name is used in the story. That is Paul Fehse. His role in the organization was to arrange meetings, direct activities, correlate information, and transmit that information to Germany. He came to the U.S. in 1934 and became a citizen in 1938. He was employed as a cook aboard ships sailing from New York Harbor.

Wilhelm Gegner is a fictitious character and was not actually one of the members of the spy ring. He is not modeled after any of the spies. And, as far as I know, Allis-Chalmers was not targeted or breached by Nazi spies.

Allis-Chalmers did, however, produce the items mentioned in the story for World War I. They also supported the efforts of World War II. In fact, 1,235 M6 high speed 38-ton tractors were built in 1944-45 at the Allis-Chalmers La Porte plant. The M6 was an artillery tractor used to move the large 240mm Howitzer, M1 8-inch gun, or the 4.7-inch gun. It was also used to tow a pair of ten-ton trailers in tandem, or other heavy loads.

Chapter 17. This chapter with Carl meeting Bill Gaines is fiction.

Chapter 18. As Germany invades Poland marking the beginning of the war, the story continues with the fictional relationship between Carl and Bill.

Chapter 19. The fiction continues, but there actually was a suspicion of those of German descent in World War II just as there had been in World War I.

Chapter 20. Carl is interviewed by the FBI. During World War I, passage of the Espionage Act of 1917 led the FBI to launch its first nationwide domestic surveillance program. As early as 1934, President Franklin D. Roosevelt tasked the FBI with overseeing intelligence operations in the entire Western Hemisphere. With the outbreak of World War II, the FBI began investigating threats to national security, including American Nazi, fascist, and communist groups.

These activities of the FBI were undertaken prior to the CIA, formed in 1947, and prior to the OSS (Office of Strategic Services), formed during World War II in 1942.

Chapters 21-29. The fictional account of Carl's story continues. The final chapter contains a summary of the outcome of the Duquesne spy ring. There were thirty-three spies arrested. All received prison sentences. None, however, were guilty of murder, and none were executed.

The statistics noted regarding Alcoholics Anonymous were the closest I could locate on the membership from about 1941. The formation of the AA group in La Porte is fictitious.

www.ingramcontent.com/pod-product-compliance
Lightning Source LLC
Chambersburg PA
CBHW050935120626
46552CB00001B/219